Surviving Sam

Surviving Sam

KAREN RIVERS

POLESTAR
An Imprint of Raincoast Books

Polestar Books and Raincoast Books gratefully acknowledge
the support of the Government of Canada through the Book
Publishing Industry Development Program, the Canada
Council and the Department of Canadian Heritage. We also
acknowledge the assistance of the Province of British Columbia
through the British Columbia Arts Council.

Edited by Lynn Henry
Cover design by Jacqueline Verkley
Cover photo © Kevin Briggs/Photonica

NATIONAL LIBRARY OF CANADA CATALOGUING IN PUBLICATION DATA
Rivers, Karen, 1970-
    Surviving Sam
    ISBN 1-55192-506-0
    I. Title.
PS8585.I8778S87 2001   jC813'.54   C2001—910862-1
PZ7.R5258Su 2001

Polestar, an Imprint of Raincoast Books
9050 Shaughnessy Street
Vancouver, British Columbia
Canada, V6P 6E5
www.raincoast.com

1 2 3 4 5 6 7 8 9 10

Printed in Canada

This book is dedicated to everyone
who has survived the impossible
and found a way to carry on.

CONTENTS

PROLOGUE

I t *all started with the trip. It was their birthday gift.
Some gift. Some birthday. Their fourteenth. They
should have had one of those parties like other kids
did. They should have played spin the bottle.*

They chose this.

*They always got things like this: trips or concert tick-
ets or adventures or lessons. They never got things, not
like their friends did. They didn't get sweaters and books
and CDs and junk. They didn't want that. If they had,
everything would have been different.*

*The hike took them across the side of a mountain. The
sun was out and they wore sunglasses to protect their
eyes from the glare, from snow blindness. The snow was
everywhere, and deep. On their feet they wore borrowed
snowshoes. Because it was so clear, the cold was like
music. It sang like middle C. It was sharp and piercing.
The top layer of snow was frozen solid. They hardly
needed the shoes, which were awkward. They walked
like baby birds, leaving splayed footprints. They could
feel the muscles in their legs burning. They were young
and strong. The wind made their skin flushed and brave.
They didn't talk. They concentrated on the terrain. To*

their right, the trail dropped off to the treetops. If I fell, Pagan thought (without really thinking), I could grab the top of a tree and hang there until rescue came.

She wasn't afraid of falling. Not then.

Behind her, she could hear Sam's footsteps crunching on the frozen snow and in front of her, her father's. In front of him was her Uncle Bob. She could see the crimson red of his parka. Red like blood. She didn't think that. She thought, red like a flag. Or a poppy. Whatever. She probably just thought: Red.

They had been walking for a while. Pagan's skin itched from being warm under her layers of clothes. She didn't complain. She wasn't the type to do that. Besides, the view was spectacular. Breathtaking. It would be hard to complain in such a beautiful place.

It was almost time to stop for lunch. She was hungry. They all were, she supposed. They had bought sandwiches at the deli in the hotel. Amazing sandwiches. They were piled high with pastrami and cheese. Her favourite. She had also purchased hot mustard in a jar when Sam wasn't looking and was carrying it in her pack. It would be a special treat. Her dad probably had a birthday cake, too, somewhere. Hidden in the depths of his pack, amongst the first-aid stuff and extra socks. Lemon cake, she thought, or hoped. That was their favourite, hers and Sam's. They liked the same things. They always had. It was a twin thing. The same food, the same sports, the same people.

Her camera banged against her chest, reminding her of what she wanted to do. She tugged the line that joined her to her father to indicate she wanted to stop. She adjusted the shutter and the camera whirred. Automatic focus. She took a picture of the lake, turquoise blue like the sky. It was miles below them, or seemed that way. It looked like a puddle or a jewel or the iris of a giant's eye. It looked small and mysterious and obscenely beautiful. They waited while she took more pictures. She turned and focused the lens on Sam. He grinned at her widely. Too widely. She could see the gap in his teeth that matched her own. It was called a diastema, her dentist told her once. She didn't want it to ever be fixed. She liked the way it was the same as Sam's. He didn't want to fix his either. If he ever did, she would reconsider. Probably. She zoomed in on it and took a picture only of his mouth. They could laugh about it later. She imagined that Mom would put it on the fridge.

They started walking again. They didn't say anything, but it was understood that they would find a good place to stop and eat. A place with a view of the lake, where they could sit without sinking down into the snow. It was cold, it felt too cold to talk. Pagan didn't mind about the view anymore. She just wanted to stop for a sandwich. Her stomach rumbled. She wanted some of that mustard. She was almost on a diet, but not quite. I'll start again tomorrow, she thought. She had a hard time with dieting because she liked food too much. She didn't want to do it — diet, that is — but her best friends Trina and Ashley were going to, so she thought she would, too. Whatever, she thought. I guess I could stand to lose a couple of pounds.

She thought about this as they walked through the perfect white snow. She thought about how Sam and his best friend Dan would tease her for dieting. Rabbit food, they'd say. Boys. They were lucky because they *could eat anything at all. She turned around and glared at him over her shoulder. He stuck out his tongue.*

She laughed.

When they first heard it, they didn't know what it was. None of them tugged on the rope, but they all stopped just the same. They looked up to their left. They should have known, should have understood. What else could it be? The sound was deafening and unmistakable. It was a sound that — even if you had never heard it before — announced what it was. There was nothing else like it.

The avalanche roared and bellowed and the sound stretched around them and surrounded them. It was an animal of unfathomable size, growling. It was a million trains, coming down a million tracks. It was everywhere. They didn't react fast enough, or really at all. There was the sound of wood snapping, which was the huge trees being plowed under.

We're going to die, Pagan thought, and she looked at Sam. She wanted to die looking at her brother. See you in heaven, she thought. See you in the next life. She tried to smile at him, and she thought he tried to smile back. He knew what she was thinking. Of course he did. She wasn't that afraid, which surprised her. She wasn't as afraid as she would have thought she would be in this situation. She was aware of that, at least. She felt very still and calm inside. Her heart beat slowly. She could feel it. She was sweating. The sweat slid off her like rain. The wall of snow was moving at incredible speed and also in slow motion. She was breathing in and out. Inhale, exhale, she thought. She could hear her father shouting instructions but she couldn't hear what they were. She hardly thought it mattered. She was paralyzed. It was like one of those dreams where you know you have to move, but you can't. At the last minute, she wished that she had moved closer to Sam. He could have held her hand or something. She could have held on to him.

She looked up at the snow that towered over her like a wave.

When it hit, it took her breath away. She was pushed up and up and down and over and she was flipped again and again. It was like being hit by a bus or a fire truck. All the air left her. Her rope pulled taut at her waist. She thought it was going to cut her in half. Her pack was torn off. She felt like she was being trampled by a herd of wild elephants. Then her head hit sharply against something, echoing for a minute. She breathed in as she passed out. In a surreal way, she was aware of her consciousness floating away. Her camera strap broke and her camera was gone. She didn't care. She was in a place that was black and hollow and wrapped around her like tar. She let it take her.

Sam, she thought, but that was all. She was gone for a while. How long? She didn't know.

She opened her eyes and it was bright again. Dazzling. She could hardly see. There was something wet and sticky on her face. That was blood. It was coming from her eye. Her sunglasses were gone. She inhaled and felt air entering her lungs and was surprised. She was alive. She was going to live. In various parts of her body, she could feel terrible pain. Pain that made her want to scream and scream and scream, but she couldn't. But she knew she wouldn't die from it. She felt certain of that. She was numb. The sky was so bright and glared down at her. Her open eye teared up and wept. It took her a while to notice that she was looking at the lake, and not the sky at all. The pain around her waist was Sam. She looked down the rope to where it went over the precipice. Sam. Sam was hanging over the edge. She couldn't move because somewhere higher up the rope, her father was anchoring her in place. Mostly, she was dangling in space herself. She opened her mouth, but all that came out was a croak.

There was something surreal and dreamlike about what was happening and it was difficult for her to put herself in the picture. There's been an avalanche, she told herself. You're alive, but you have to move. Or you are going to freeze to death.

Experimentally, she wiggled her fingers and toes. It hurt. God, did it hurt.

"Sam," she said. The silence in contrast to the roar of the avalanche was overwhelming. It was like being inside an echo. She toyed with the idea that she had been deafened, but she had heard her own voice quite clearly. The rope tightened from one side to another. Sam must be swinging, she thought. She tried not to move, to still the rope.

She tried again. "Dad," she said.

"Sam. Dad."

"Pagan," her dad said. "Don't move."

His voice was strange and far away.

"I'm trying to ... It's your Uncle Bob," he said. "He ..."

Uncle Bob was dead, she supposed. She couldn't see him but she could guess from her dad's voice. She felt sad but still not scared. Later, she'd see him, and the fear would curl around her like a snake, tightening. His neck was broken and he was lying in the snow staring up at the blue blue sky with hollow eyes.

A raven flew overhead and called out. She heard that.

Quoth the raven, nevermore, she thought. That was from English class. Edgar Allan Poe. It seemed very odd and impossible that she had ever sat in a classroom and read poetry. She was upside down and hanging on a steep ledge. She couldn't see Sam. She pressed her legs into the snow that seemed to support her. It creaked and crumbled. Chunks of it fell past her into nothingness.

"Sam," she said again, louder.

"Sam. Sam!"

"Pagan?"

"Sam."

"I'm ..."

"Sam?"

She felt him go, more than she heard him. He didn't make a sound. She felt the rope loosening, but also something more. She felt something falling inside her. It was like that moment when you fall asleep and sometimes you have the sensation of really falling. It was like that, only it went on and on. She couldn't have imagined anything like it until it happened. It was like dying, or so she imagined.

Sam

Sam

Sam.

No no no no no no no.

But of course, he had fallen. He fell. Quietly. He didn't scream. That was Pagan, of course.

Pagan was left alone. She held on to the rope that had held him. She pulled it towards her and inspected the end. It was cut neatly, as though by a knife. She put the end of the rope in her mouth. It tasted salty and charred.

Sam.

"Dad?" she said. "Dad?"

"Pagan, hang on."

"Dad," she said. "Sam fell."

They were rescued. Pagan and her father. She would never forget the chopper blades cutting heavily through the empty sky. From the air, they saw the side of the mountain heave again. The second avalanche blew past the place where they had been. If they had still been there, they all would have died.

They said Sam fell into the lake. That was all very well, but they never found his body.

Never.

He was just gone.

fall

CHAPTER 1

September is the worst month. No, January is worse. Because of my birthday. Our birthday, or what would have been our birthday. If we'd lived. Well, I lived, obviously, but it's not the same. It's the anniversary, too. The anniversary of Sam's death. This January, I'll be seventeen.

September is hard for different reasons. After the nothingness of summer vacation, all the time spent lying on the lawn, lying on my bed, lying on the beach, I have to get up. I have to move around like a normal person. I have to go back to pretending. The hard part has to do with school and it has to do with going to school without Sam. You'd think I'd be past it, right? I mean, three years. Where were you three years ago? Do you even remember?

It's been almost three years since I last saw Sam. They tell me he's dead. Do they think I don't know? I went with him, I know where he's gone. But still I tell my psychiatrist, Dr. Killian, that maybe he's not dead. I mean, they never found the body. Maybe he found some way to live underwater. Maybe there was a fissure in the earth that he fell through and is now existing in some other layer of the planet, taken in by a lost people some-how. A lost tribe. Maybe they made him king, and maybe he is worshipped by millions. Maybe.

Or maybe he is just worshipped by me.

"No," Dr. Killjoy tells me. "No, Pagan. Sam is dead."

I think that is what the sessions are all about: him telling me that Sam is dead. Over and over and over again. As if there is a finite number of times I need to hear it before I'll believe it.

I know he is dead. I know. I know. I know it more than I know anything else. It's bigger than I am, Sam's death. It's taken me over. I only say that he isn't to make con-versation. To fill these stupid sessions with what-ifs. There are things I can't say. Things I don't have the words for. Like how, inside me, there is a giant hollow space where he once was. It is black and cold and empty, full of cracks and fine breaks, like that old china Grandma uses. A lace web of tiny scars. It is a void, a vacuum.

It is inside of me and yet it is more than me. I don't know how to explain it right, but that's how it feels.

When Sam fell, I hung on to the ledge for four hours before the rescue team swooped in, hammering the silence to bits with their machines, leaving it shattered. My hands were frostbitten. I still have scars there, scars like lace that I trace over and over again with my fin-gernail, with my pen, with whatever is in my hand. The scars themselves have no feelings. I can hardly feel the piano keys when I play, or the guitar strings, or the keys on the clarinet. I think some people react to death differently, and form a scar over their heart. I wish I had one of those, like my mom does. A scar so big and horrible that I could just become completely numb.

Without feelings. Running on automatic pilot through each predictable step of the grieving process. Like Mom. I just want to stop feeling his loss. I do.

And yet I don't. I don't want to let him go.

I broke my ribs, my leg, and both of my arms. I was shattered from the inside out. It took a year for them to glue my body back together. Each time they put me under for another operation, I prayed not to wake up. I meant it. I wasn't kidding. Mom and Dad would be sitting by the bed when I woke up, and I could see that they were relieved. They were depending on me to wake up each time. And I saw something else, too. Something more like anger. I didn't want to understand. I had enough to deal with on my own. They could take care of themselves.

Me, me, me. My shrink says I'm too self-involved. What does he know? On his desk, there is a picture of a beautiful woman who must be his wife. She has hair down to her waist. In the picture, she is holding a puppy. I imagine that someone like him cannot possibly understand someone like me.

Sometimes I look back on the day of the accident and I wonder why I didn't let go. I could have released the rope. I could have fallen with him. We would still be together. You have to understand: Sam and I were born together. We were formed at the same time, accidentally. My parents were together before they got married, and here we are. Or there we were. Now "we" is just "me." I'll never get used to that. My parents still aren't married, to tell you the truth. But no one knows that. They have the same last name and everything. My mom changed hers to be the same as his. Me and Sam already had his name, we were born with it: Riddler.

We were conceived and developed at the *same time*. Our thoughts were the same, our first words. We even breathed in synch. I tell the psychiatrist that and he doesn't believe me. I can tell he doesn't because he smiles at me, pityingly. I don't need pity. I hate pity. Pity fills me up with a white hot rage that I can't contain. One day, I'll let it out and it will explode from me like a bird of prey, tearing up everything in its path. My pain is a monster. Pity doesn't save me.

I need Sam.

My bones have healed. I do all the same sports that I used to do. It was all part of the endless physio: the moving of my body through the motions, the lifting of all the heavy weights, the rebuilding, redefining of my muscles. I am a better athlete than I ever was before. I'm perfect. Although there is still a lump if you feel my ribs. You can even see it, if I stand in a certain way. When I lie in bed, I touch it. It is the lump I got when Sam fell. I touch it and I touch it and I touch it and I try to bring him back. At night, I fall asleep and I dream that he is still here, or worse, I dream that he is gone.

Sometimes I even dream that I am sleeping and he is sleeping in same room and I can hear our harmonized breaths. When I dream like that, I wake up confused to find him not here. But for a split second before the confusion sets in, the room is bathed in sunlight and I think, I'll get up now. It's morning. Thoughts a normal person might have. And then I remember that Sam fell. And I sink back down under the covers and into the quicksand of sleep. I try to get back to Sam, to the part in the dream where he was still alive. Dr. Killjoy says that people who are depressed tend to sleep too much or too little. I sleep too much, according to him, and so I am depressed. No, I tell him. My brother died, and I'm not depressed. I'm in mourning.

I will be in mourning forever.

Someone found my camera in the spring, when the snow had melted. It was destroyed, of course. I think of the last picture I took and wish I could get it back. I can almost imagine what it would look like. It is the ghost of an image in my mind, not quite real enough to see. I pray for it. I hold the mangled film and wish for it. I would sell my soul for that picture. I would, if anyone wanted it. I keep that ruined film with me all the time. I'm always waiting for someone or something that can magically restore it.

Two and three-quarters years is a long time and also no time at all. I can remember everything about that day, but almost nothing of the day before and the day after and all the days after that that have made up two and a half years of being alone.

My mom tells me not to dwell on it, to move on. "Time heals all wounds," she says. She is full of sayings that mean nothing to me, and I wonder how she can say that. She lost a son. She gets her ideas — her "methods of coping" — from this group that she belongs to, some group of sad people who get together once a week to talk about their dead kids. The thing is, though, that she seems to forget she has a kid who is still alive. Me. I went with her to that group, once. I didn't belong. Their grief was different than mine. It was public grief, and it all looked like an act. Choreographed and rehearsed. Mine is deep inside. Mine is different. It's raw and rough and ugly. They all held hands around a circle and read poetry and talked about love and survival. My mom says that she's a survivor and that she is strong. Ha. What did she survive? She wasn't there. The rope wasn't around her waist. She didn't feel it when it gave way.

My father has reacted more normally. He has become uglier. Alternately cold and angry, and overly warm and friendly. I wonder what he is doing, but I'm not sure I have the energy to care. Is he drinking too much in the bar after work? Where does he go? Is it an old man's pub or a stripper bar? Does my dad ogle naked women to make himself feel better? Is he cheating on Mom, on both of us? He is staying late at the office, but I know it isn't the office because he comes home red-eyed and smelling like smoke. I don't care that he smokes. I smoke, too, but I care that he's hiding it, that he does it in secret. I think that he's spineless and that he's weak. And I hate him. I hate him for doing the obvious things. I hate Mom for not noticing.

I hate everyone.

No doubt Dad would say he is doing it to get away from the hippie-freak love of my mom and her "group," to get away from me and my endless sobbing. I know I should do something about this. Maybe I should tell Mom, or maybe she already knows, but I can't bring myself to get involved. Whatever, I think. I hate him, but I sort of applaud him for lashing out, for doing something. My mother has whisked it all away and wrapped it up in a neat bundle that she brings out once a week for her group and then packs up again until the next time. I just let mine consume me.

We're all screwed up, the three of us. Our griefs are all too different to live in one house together. Three different species existing on three different planes.

I have nurtured mine to the point where it has taken me over and drowned me and killed me a hundred times.

I am surprised that I am still alive.

In the last two and a half years, I have tried to kill myself eight times. Are you surprised? It was the only thing I knew to do to rid myself of my monstrous white hot pain. I have taken bottles of pills and poisons, swallowing and swallowing and swallowing. But I always wake up. My parents only count the two times that I bled. The other six were pills that I ended up throwing up, voluntarily or into a pump that sucked me dry. All those times I went to sleep and didn't think I'd wake up. The relief of it all. And then there I was, awake. It's a joke. I can't even die. Every day, there I am: Mom knocking at my door and telling me to get up for school. I can't believe they don't notice the black circles under my eyes, the look I have of being nearly gone. I want them to notice. I want them to leave me alone.

I tried seriously. Twice. With razors. I used the steel to release the pain. I had to. Sharp silver blades that split my skin like lips, parting to say something. Opening to talk. It hurt, oh God, it hurt. I did it. I felt so calm at first. I thought I meant it, but I got scared in a way that I hadn't been when I faced the wall of snow. I'll admit that. When the water in the tub turned pink, then red, I was scared. It smelled like metal. My mom found me both times. Her eyes wide and horrified. I'll never forget the look on her face, even though I was only half awake, half alive, half there. It's the only time I've seen her drop her mask. The first time, she threw up. It was unexpected, I guess. Shocking. A new grief. She threw up before she called for help. I wanted to tell her that it was okay, but I couldn't talk. That was when I was fifteen. One year after Sam died, almost to the day. I just couldn't take it anymore. I couldn't. The next month when I did it again, she was calmer. She knew what to do. I don't even know why I did it, that second time. Just to see if it was going to take, I guess. Just to test my ability to die.

Now I have bracelets of scars around my wrists and ankles. I have had three different psychiatrists. The man I see now is named Dr. Killian. I told you that. I call him Dr. Killjoy, which upsets him. I think that's why I keep going back, to taunt him. Or maybe he helps me. I don't know. I don't think anyone can help me. His office smells like lavender and mint. I think he is trying to use aromatherapy to cure me without telling me. I think he pumps in different fragrances to disarm me of Sam.

Sam repellents.

I am going to see Dr. Killjoy this afternoon, after school. It is six in the morning right now and I am lying in bed under plaid flannel sheets. Boy's sheets. Sam's sheets. They are soft and warm and I kick my feet around to find a cool place. If I can find just the right spot, maybe I'll be able to get back to sleep. I rub the lump on my rib and think about the day ahead. It's too much. I am overwhelmed by the idea of getting up and showering and getting dressed and eating and walking up the street and getting to the right classroom at the right time.

Every day, it is so hard. It is almost impossible.

Every day, I try. I do.

Before Sam fell, I used to leap from bed every morning so that I could sneak in to wake him up. He was always up already. We would fight over the shower and what to make for breakfast and we would walk to school together. It was a different school, so we walked down the street instead of up. Now I go to the senior high school on the other side of the neighbourhood. Alone.

This is my last year of school. We were the gifted twins, skipped over the first grade together. I'll graduate alone.

Sam and I walked to school together every day, unless one of us was sick. We took all the same classes. We were on all the same teams: swimming, track, volleyball, soccer. We had all the same friends: Trina, Ashley and Dan. We played in our own band. We thought we were going to grow up together and then become famous musicians or athletes. We hadn't decided which. I was a better athlete, and he was a better musician. That's the truth. That's the way it was.

When I walk to school now, I feel alone and afraid. I have been afraid on and off since Sam died, but after the wrist cutting, it changed. I started to have panic attacks, or so my shrink says. I started forgetting how to breathe, jumping at the tiniest noise, avoiding going out in case I panicked. Now I am always looking over my shoulder. The neighbourhood is quiet and suburban and sometimes I'll see a deer running across someone's yard, clip-clopping across the street in front of me. Occasionally, a dog will bark at me, or someone will pass by on a bicycle. I'll see other kids walking to school. There is nothing scary here, no low rumbling sounds of mountains giving way to open space. A car alarm goes off and I almost jump out of my skin.

I try to keep all those feelings inside, so no one can see how crazy I really am.

At school, I am a different person. I try to be. I'm not fooling anyone. Kids avoid me. There is something they can see in me, a horror that runs so deep that I repel people. I smile and laugh and gossip just enough to not be a freak. I'll talk about the other kids or the teachers or something that happened on TV. I get so tired after talking. I hate it. I don't have friends. Not close ones. I keep busy so I don't have to talk. I soar along just over the surface of all that happens, slightly above and apart from the crowd. All the while, I watch myself as though from a great distance. I see myself starting to blend in, and I lurch inside. I float away from it all to where I can find Sam. Together, *we* watch *me*. It's all a performance. I never feel like smiling or laughing or gossiping. At the end of the day, I am exhausted.

I don't know who I am anymore.

I still play sports and music. I do all the same things. I don't want Sam to think that I stopped doing what he loved. I do more and more so that I don't have time to stop and think. I have trouble eating and staying awake, and sometimes I think I am only on those teams because the coaches know about Sam and they feel sorry for me. I am not nearly as good an athlete as I used to be. Physical strength has nothing to do with it. My heart isn't in it anymore. I have no passion left for anyone or anything. Once, I raced just to feel the pull of my own muscles and I felt strong and crazy powerful. I felt like I could run or swim or play forever, like I could do anything. Now, I feel like I am trying to run under a heavy weight. I feel like I can barely put one foot in front of the next, much less sprint or throw my body over an aluminum pole. I have become glued to the ground. Grief is gravity. I have more than my share.

I am almost seventeen. I am no one. Who am I? Am I only what I look like? A shell. I am an average-looking girl. I look like someone that you think you know. So bland that I disappear, or I would if it weren't for my eye. Or my lack of eye, I guess you could say. I only have one eye, now, although I used to have two. I lost one in the accident. The Accident, capital letters. I lost my eye and my brother. I don't care that much about my eye, although I hate it that it makes me stand out. I hate the eye patch. I like summer so that I can wear sunglasses and slip away behind them. I am tall and gangly and small-breasted. I have long hair that is light brown or blondish and mousy and hangs to my waist. I haven't cut it since Sam died. If I smile in the mirror, I can still see the gap in my teeth and then there he is. Sam. He is right beneath my skin, scratching to get out. A fourteen-year-old boy trapped in a sixteen-year-old girl's body, in her heart.

He is in me, in the mirror. I can't shake it.

Time doesn't heal anything. My mom can shove that little gem up her ass. I am not healed. My bones are healed, but I am broken. I have fallen into a bottomless lake and I don't know how to get out. I don't even know if I want to anymore.

Seven a.m. I get up out of bed. Big deal, right? I can't tell you how big of a deal it is to me. Every day. The wood floors are cold on my feet, but I hardly feel it. I mean, I can tell it's cold, but it seems too far away to care about. I stare at the clothes in the closet and skip the shower. I choose jeans and a sweater and socks and shoes and underwear and arrange them on my body so people will think I am normal. I put on some makeup and brush my hair and my teeth and I make breakfast. By "make breakfast" I mean I wash an apple and polish it slowly on a dish towel until it gleams, and then I eat it. Since Sam died, I have been unable to eat anything soft or richly flavoured. I will only eat food that crunches cleanly against my teeth, food with a strong, specific taste: sour or flat. It's all I can swallow. I swear. Everything else makes me sick.

Mom and Dad are still in bed when I leave the house. They must be able to hear me as I wander around the kitchen but they don't come in. They think I need time to myself, maybe, or maybe they find it hard to wake up in the morning, too. I don't know. I sure don't ask.

I leave the house and slam the door behind me, to make sure they wake up. If I don't get to sleep late, then neither should they, right?

The sidewalk is still wet with dew. I point myself in the direction of school and walk, one foot after another. While I walk, I listen to the irregular tick-tock of my heart and feel my pulse with one finger. My rhythm skips and jumps. There is something wrong with me today, something more wrong than usual. I'm having trouble catching my breath. Last night, I dreamed of Sam, flying. I dreamed of me, falling. When I don't sleep soundly,

I wake up dizzy, like I am now. The ground tilts and lurches and tilts again. I stop walking and stare at the wet sidewalk. There is a puddle building by the grate, blocked by a scab of leaves. The pavement is grey and solid. I press my fingers harder into my wrist and feel my pulse changing. I remind myself to breathe, to calm down. And then I think, oh, why bother. Why bother with this? I look up at the sky and feel a pain radiating from my chest to my shoulder. A big pain. It splits me open. The sky ricochets and slips out of focus. There is no one around when I fall. I hit my head as I faint, gently, like an afterthought. Like I'm doing it on purpose.

A flurry of feet and voices wakes me up, just as I am sliding from darkness and into a dream. Strangers' feet, at least I hope so. I would die if they were the feet of someone I knew, someone from school. Then they would know how crazy I am, then everyone would know. That's the game — to keep it a secret. That's what I've learned. Craziness scares people. They don't know what to do with it. With you. You learn to hide it. A blanket drops down over me and faces come into and out of focus. I close my eyes. Go away, I think. Leave me the hell alone. The sirens scream down the street. A fat man in a uniform starts asking questions, taking my pulse, peering into my eye. I can feel myself blushing, I can feel the heat of my humiliation crawling down my throat. I sit up.

"I'm fine," I say. "Oops. Just fine, I …"

I push the blanket off me. It is such a pretty blanket, pink and white. A baby's blanket. It looks so incongruous there on the wet sidewalk. I reach up and tap on my patch to assure myself it's still there. I stare at the people with my good eye.

"I'll just go," I say, standing.

No, no, no. No such luck. I will myself to separate from this insane scene: the oxygen mask clamped over my nose, the stretcher that reminds me so much of other stretchers and other times, the scenery slipping by through the upside-down window of the racing ambulance.

In Emergency, a doctor checks me over. Listens to my heart, which is now loping along like a fat dog. Stares into my eyes. Asks me questions. Takes my blood. I lie there quietly and watch through a crack in the curtains as people come and go. There is a certain sense of suspended animation here, the people are all trapped with their pain until a doctor can get to them, and even then there is no guarantee that he or she can do anything to help. I wonder how many of these people are faking it for the attention. For half a second I wonder if I am faking it, too. But I did faint. That wasn't fake. Everyone here is old except me, but inside I am older than they are. They have no idea. I am ancient, ageless, older than life. I am ragged inside, and as old as mountains. As white as snow.

When the doctor finally comes back, he has a milk moustache above his top lip, just out of reach of his flicking tongue. He is reptilian. His eyes are sharp and black. I can't imagine him slumping down in the break room, tossing back a glass of milk before returning to the madness of this emergency room. Milk. He even has acne. How old is he? Nineteen? Twenty? How old do you have to be to doctor people? If I were an emergency room doctor, I'd probably be sneaking out back for a cigarette, at least. I glare at him, to make him know that I know who he really is: a smart kid, a geek, a nerd. Aren't all doctors just the smart kids all grown up?

I used to think I wanted to be a doctor. I was a smart kid myself. I am a smart kid. Now the idea of being anything is just too tiring to even think about. I want to be nothing. I want to just stop.

"Pagan," he says, pronouncing it wrong, giving the 'g' a soft 'j' sound. "Pagan, I think you had a panic attack."

"Ha," I say. "No."

"Yes," he says. "I think so."

"No," I tell him. "I've had panic attacks. I know what they are. They are different. I wasn't scared this time. It wasn't scary. I just fainted. Maybe I was hungry. But I had a pain in my chest. It could be a heart attack."

"Maybe," he says. "Maybe you were hungry. What did you eat for breakfast?"

I don't answer because I can tell he is losing interest. An old lady in the cubicle next to me screams, "Tell my husband to eat his goddamn prunes and then this wouldn't happen!"

The doctor sighs and shrugs. He looks tired and too young for this. "Panic attack," he says again. "That explains the chest pain. Is there someone you can see about it?"

"I have a shrink," I say. "He'll fix me right up." I say it as sarcastically as I can, but he doesn't flinch. He just notes something on my chart — probably something about how "difficult" I am — and hangs it back on its hook and walks away. His shoes squeak on the floor.

An hour later, my dad shows up to pick me up. He looks sad, stretched to the limit. "Panic attack, huh?" he says.

"Try a heart attack," I tell him.

"Have you had them before?" he says, adjusting the volume on the radio so he can hear me, or at least so he can pretend to be interested.

"Heart attacks?" I say. "Sure, every day."

"Panic attacks," he says. "Pagan."

"What?" I say. I turn up the volume on the radio and then change the station. I turn it up as loud as I dare, and he lets me. My parents let me do all kinds of things now. It's like they are afraid not to. I'm glass. Handle with care. They don't want to be responsible for the irreparable shattering.

"I have them all the time," I say, when I know the music is too loud for him to hear me. He isn't listening. He stares down the road as though there might be something really interesting just around the corner.

It's true. That I have them all the time. Panic attacks. But they're different. They are different each time. They shouldn't call them panic attacks. Panic isn't always a component. Sometimes it's just a pain in your heart that is too much for you to bear.

I spend the morning back in bed, listening to the silence in the house, the dripping pipes, the footsteps of a bird on the roof. The crows, screaming. Once, this symphony of quiet noise is broken by the ringing phone, and my mom's voice on the tape, checking to see if I'm all right. She's getting pizza for dinner, she says, as though I'll care. As though I'll eat it. As though I'm ten years old and excited by a slab of cheese and fatty meat. She won't come home and check on me because she is probably scared that I'll be in the tub again. I don't think she could face it. In a way, I know how she feels. When we were kids, Sam and me, we had pet guinea pigs, Boris and Annabelle. Boris was mine. He was black and long haired. One day Sam went downstairs to get Annabelle to take her outside to play on the grass and she was dead. Just lying there. I'll never forget it, the way that he screamed. After that, I was scared to look at Boris. I loved him, but I didn't want him to be dead, so I stopped going down there. I paid Sam to clean his cage, and we stopped playing with him and taking him out-side to eat the grass on the lawn. I stopped holding him and listening to him squeak. It was stupid, I know it. He died pretty soon after that. I didn't see him dead. He died when we were away and the house sitter buried him before we got home.

In the afternoon, I make myself get up and take a cab to see Dr. Killian. I'm scared to walk to the bus stop and get on and faint in front of people and have to go through the whole emergency room melodrama again. I'm scared of embarrassing myself. The cab costs $10, which is all that I have, so I'll have to walk home. It isn't that far if I cut through the park. Maybe Dr. Killjoy will cure me in this session and walking home won't be a problem. I go into his office and sit on the leather chair and wait for him to draw it out of me. He doesn't. I don't know how to bring it up, so instead I stare at the picture of his perfect girlfriend and perfect puppy and I trace the scars on my wrist and I wait. Finally he says, "How was school?" And I start to cry, because that is what Mom and Dad should ask me, over dinner or whatever, like they used to, like other people's parents do, and instead they don't say much of anything, and I don't say anything, and I hate Dr. Killjoy for saying it. He's a stranger. He's a stranger that is paid to listen to my crying, paid to offer me a tissue, paid to ask me if I feel like talking about it.

I force myself to stop crying, and I stare out his window and count passing cars until the end of the session. As I get ready to leave, to walk home, he says, "The pills are still an option."

I glower at him. "I'll think about it," I say, like I always do. But I don't want to take his stupid pills. I just want to be normal. Only crazy people take pills. I don't want to be crazy. I know I am, but I don't want to be a crazy person who takes pills. That's crossing a line I've made for myself in the sand. Besides, I know about Prozac. It's everywhere, isn't it? It's trendy. I don't know if a trendy pill is the answer to anything.

I saw a show once about a vet who gave Prozac to animals in his practice. Neurotic animals. There was this one dog that wouldn't give up this old, rotten stick. It would go crazy if the stick was out of sight for a second, barking and howling and moaning like a person. It was pathetic and awful, but at the same time it was funny. It was totally absurd. The dog could absolutely not get over the fact he lost his stupid stick. So they gave this crazy dog some Prozac, and he walked away from that old thing. He couldn't have cared less about it, that hunk of wood that he used to love so much. Really. That show made me sad.

What I am afraid of is that the pills will take Sam away from me. That the pills will make me happy and Sam will become a memory and the black place inside me will be filled and I will stop collapsing in the street and stop needing to have my head shrunk and stop being so sad. I don't want to walk away from Sam like he's an old hunk of dirty wood. Does that make sense?

I've done the research. I don't care much about the chemicals, the long-term effects, any of that. It's more than just that. What if I get a Prozac personality? Hyper and happy all the time. I don't want to be happy. That's the truth. Maybe I don't choose happiness. How can I be happy? My brother is dead. I want to scream it from the rooftops. I want everyone to know.

I want everyone to care.

I want to be normal, but I don't deserve to be.

I guess you can see that I don't know what I want. I don't know how to be anyone. Maybe I should take the pills. Maybe. I might try them, this time. It's been almost three years.

Maybe it's time I let Sam go.

CHAPTER 2

The next day, I call Dan. I don't know why. I haven't talked to him since the funeral. He was Sam's friend. I kind of changed my friends so that I wouldn't have to talk about anything with them. I traded them all in for people who didn't know me well enough to care, enough to notice my craziness. To notice how different I am. I dial the number, which I still know off by heart. The phone is slippery in my hand. What am I doing? I think. Dan isn't even my friend now. He wasn't really even my friend Before. He was just there. He was there with Sam.

The phone rings and rings and rings, but no one answers. In a way, I'm relieved. I go into the music room and start playing my guitar. It's a beautiful instrument. Amber wood, softly shaped. It fits perfectly in my arms, like it was meant to be there, even back when it was just a tree I imagine that I would have loved it. This guitar means everything to me. The strings are an extension of my fingers. The chords are my voice. When I play, I don't have to think about the music, the music just happens. But I can think about other stuff. About Dan and Sam and the way we used to hang out here. Before and before and before. I always think about Before, never about After.

Before: what was it like before? Did it even happen? I remember it like I remember books that I've read. Like it wasn't me, but just a character printed out on a page in black and white. My character was happy. I didn't even think about it, that's how happy I was. Why would I? I liked myself. I didn't look in the mirror and flinch and look away. I didn't shake all the time. I didn't know what it was like to always be afraid, or to be afraid at all. I wouldn't have understood people like the person I am now. I had a narrow, happy frame of reference. So you see how this experience has made me a more well-rounded person.

That's a joke.

We used to always joke around, me and Sam and Mom and Dad and whoever was around. We always had friends over. Ashley, Trina, Dan. They all used to say we were such a cool family. I can picture all of us crowded around the table. But that was a long time ago, the picture is fading. Melting. All the colours are running together and I can't pick out our faces anymore. I can't hear our voices. We had a whole series of stupid routines we could go into, where we had fake accents and pretended to be different people. We're the Riddlers, after all. "We have a reputation to uphold," we used to say.

Ha.

"We should take this act on the road," Sam said.

Here's a riddle: who is half missing, half blind, half dead and half crazy?

Here's the answer: Pagan Riddler.

I've lost it. Nothing is funny. Funny died with Sam. People sure don't want to hang around like they used to. Who can blame them? Not me. I don't blame anyone for anything. I don't want to be here either. This house is too crowded with sadness and anger and simmering rage, just below the dusty surface. It's all ugly. When I lost my eye, it just made me look on the outside like I already looked inside. Half missing. My left eye was green, like the right. It is still green in a milky way, but I can't see anything through it. It stares off to one side, as though looking for something. Or someone. (Sam, always Sam.) I look strange. Ugly.

I feel strange and ugly.

I've forgotten something. Packed it away tight, and I can't recall what it was. Something about how to live. Something about how to look forward and not always back.

I sometimes wish that I could close my right eye, too, hide it behind a black patch so that I don't have to see how normal and happy everyone else is. I can't remember how to make jokes about this, about anything. Maybe it's just that I used to think things were funny when they weren't. Just things on TV. Things that we did. Sam and I would sit in the kitchen after school, before Mom and Dad got home, and we'd make prank calls. We'd call people and ask for famous people. Like the President. We'd say, "It's an emergency! I know he's there! Put him on immediately, or … aaaargghghh!" We'd scream and hang up. Stupid. It was just kid stuff. But we'd laugh and laugh and laugh like our bodies were going to explode from laughing. It was just fun, that's all. Stupid fun.

I put down the guitar. I sit on the floor, cross-legged. The room is quiet. Choked with dust. From here I can see the layers of it, settled on every surface. Dust is mostly flakes of skin. How old is this dust? Is it all me? I am completely and totally alone. I pick up the phone again and dial a random number.

"Hello?" someone says.

"I'm sorry," I say. "Wrong number."

I do it again and again. But it doesn't make me laugh. I feel a headache starting behind my missing eye and I go into the kitchen for Tylenol. It's the only pill that's around, to tell you the truth. Everything else has been hidden away. After all, you never know when old Pagan might go crazy again, do you?

Right after The Accident, things started happening to my body — apart from my desire to leave my body behind. My doctor says the changes are "hysterical." I thought that word went out of use about a hundred years ago. Hysterical? It doesn't matter what they call it, I guess, it still affects me the same way. It doesn't go away. I have developed lumps on my legs, under the skin, that felt as though they were attached to the bone. My stomach stopped being able to digest food, and if I was not throwing up, I was hunched on the toilet, praying for death to stop the pain of the cramping. I got dizzy. Not the normal kind of dizzy, the round and round feeling, but an end-over-end dizzy. Somersaulting through space, untethered. I got headaches and blurred vision. A Vaseline shield that covered up all the harsh edges. That was real, they said. That was scar tissue from the head injury.

I think it's sadness. They can call it scar tissue. I don't care.

I think it's fear. I'm scared every minute of my life. This minute.

"Inhale, exhale," I say. "Inhale, exhale."

"Sam is dead," I say. No one can hear me. I say it again. The words splash from my mouth like tiny white birds and fill the room with down. I lie back and watch them soar through the thick cloud of air that I struggle to inhale. Sam. Is. Dead. Is. Sam. Dead. Sam. Is. The floor in here is wood. My exhalations make wind patterns in the dust.

It only just happened. It happened thirty-one months ago. It's not okay to talk about it anymore. I want to talk about him, I want to do nothing but talk about him, but no. It's not okay. My parents want me to stop. To stop skulking around the house, sliding around the walls like a shadow. To stop sleeping all the time. To stop being sick and listening to my pulse and counting my breaths against the kitchen timer. They want me to get over it so that they can get over it. They want to stop seeing Sam in me. They want me to stop.

Mom says, "Deal with it."

Deal with it. That's funny. I guess she means for me to deal with it like she does, which is to have a hippie love fest about it with strangers, vomiting up her bilious grief in public once a week over tea and cookies. I wonder what she says there. I wonder if she ever says, "I wish it was Pagan who fell." Her group would even be able to make that acceptable. Turn it into a Hallmark card of anger printed on a flowery background in calligraphy.

I can't do what she does.

I can't and I can't and I can't.

I can't do anything.

I'm sorry. I am scratching and clawing, but I can't get out of my own head. This is what it sounds like in my crazy skull all the time, the white bowl of bone cups around all the what-ifs, all the possibilities. They play off every surface, like my bone is a slide projector that won't shut off. The memories leak out through the crack, though. Memories are dust, too fine to grasp. Crazy talk, crazy thoughts. It never never never stops.

I get up off the floor and kick the guitar. It spins in place on the floor. I go out of the house and walk slowly down the sidewalk. Panic flaps loosely in my chest, to remind me. I don't feel like I'm going to faint, but I keep my finger on my pulse just in case. The sidewalk is steep. I step on all the cracks. I pass by my old friend Ashley's house. It's dusk, and I can see lights on in her bedroom and someone moving around in there. I miss her. When I see her in the hallways at school I avoid her. On purpose. I don't know why. I can't talk to her. I want to. I want to tell her how great she looks, how her hair suits her, or ask her where she got her sweater or something, anything, but each time I try to talk, feathers fill my throat. I have no voice. I open my mouth and a small curl of soft whiteness floats out. I duck and hide so that I don't start to cry. It's stupid, I know. She was my best friend. When we were kids. Before and before and before. Not now. I keep walking. I walk and I walk. It feels okay.

"I am okay," I say. "I am."

The air is fresh and gentle. The leaves are just starting to change, small flickers of flame in the green foliage. I pull my lighter out of my pocket and flick the flame against my thumb. I light a cigarette and walk with it between my lips, breathing in on it like a snorkel.

I find myself outside the mall. The mall is an affront, an insult amongst all the trees and soft-coloured homes. The parking lot blazes with acidic light. I let my cigarette drop to the ground. I go in. The air is fake and sterile and hard to breathe. It's nearly deserted. I feel safer when there is no one around. I think about calling home but I don't do it. I want them to worry. I do it on purpose. Or I don't. The pay phones blink accusingly at me as I pass, a row of silver parents waiting to be alerted. I wish I could breathe. I go into a store, into a store that sells those short shirts that all the popular girls wear to show off their belly button rings. The music is loud and fills me up. I flip through a rack. Flip, flip, flip. Everything is the same. Can anyone tell that I am crazy? Do I look normal? I examine a price tag. Hold a shirt up to the light. My heart drums in my ears and the music breathes so I don't have to. No one asks if they can help me.

There is a girl next to me with a bar through her nose and earrings in her eyebrow. One of them is infected and scabbed. She looks calm. My hands are shaking. She looks at me and raises her eyebrow, the clean one. She laughs. As she gets closer, I can smell her. She smells like beer and incense and sex. I back away. The salesgirl catches my eye and grimaces. She is watching the girl with the piercings, I can tell. She thinks that she is a shoplifter, I guess, her silver studs flashing a warning.

For a second, I am furious. My hand pulls a T-shirt from a hanger and crumples it up small. So small, impossibly small. It goes into my purse. I leave the store, sweating, a cool mask of moisture on my lip that I lick away. It tastes of salt. Behind me, the pierced girl clears her throat.

"I saw that," she says.

I ignore her. I walk. Inhale, exhale. Left, right. People pass me with arms laden down with bags. Normal people. What do normal people buy? How can they walk by me without seeing that I'm a fake, a fraud? I don't belong.

Crazy me.

In the tiled washroom, the floor is wet and festooned with unwound toilet paper. Shit floats in an unflushed toilet. People leave their revolting remainders. It stinks. I sit on the counter and lean on the paper towel dispenser. Behind me, in the mirror, I do the same. I unroll the T-shirt from my purse. It's tiny. Do normal people wear clothes this small? In glittery letters across the chest, it says Porn Star. I put it back in my purse. I take it out of my purse and put it in the garbage. I take it out of the garbage and put it back in my purse. I take off my sweatshirt. In the mirror, I am naked from the waist up. I hope someone comes in. I hope they don't. I put the T-shirt on, knocking my sweatshirt to the floor. Its sleeve touches the toilet. I throw it away. The mirror is filthy. In it, I glare back at myself, the sparkling words flashing on my faded chest.

I look like a slut.

Sam, I think. *Please save me from myself.*

In the department store on my way to the exit, I pass

through rows and rows of lawnmowers. A man is arguing with his son.

"I'm not buying a goddamn gas lawnmower," he
says. "Electric or nothing."

"I'm the one who mows the lawn," the son says. "I
don't like electric mowers."

My head jerks around. I know that voice.

"I'm buying the fucking mower," the father says.
"I'll choose it."

"Fuck you," the son says.

The son.

"Dan," I say. I cross my arms over my chest. His
father leers at me.

"Well," he says. "Pagan Riddler. All grown up."

"Hi," I say. Dan's face is red. He looks down at his
shoe. Behind him, through the glass doors, I can see
that it is dark.

"Pagan," Dan says. "Want to go for coffee?"

"Um," I say.

"Don't look at me," his dad says, suddenly all smiles.
"I'm just gonna buy this mower and I'm out of here.
You kids go on." I see Dan wince. Is it the word "kids"?

"I called you," I say. "Before."

"Before when?" he says. He looks at me strangely. His
eyes drift down to my chest. I pull my hair forwards.

"Earlier," I say. "It doesn't matter."

"Why did you phone me?" he says.

"Forget it," I say. "You know, I don't really drink
coffee. I should get going. You should ... you go without me."

"I don't want to go without you," he says. "Don't
be stupid."

I put my hand on the glass door. I start to leave. He grabs my arm and his fingers give me shocks.

"Sorry," he says. "I really want to go for coffee. With you. Please. I'd like a friend right now."

"I'm not your friend," I say. "You don't even know me."

"You called me," he says. "And I do know you," he adds.

"Yes," I say. "You probably do." A tiny feather drifts from my lip and floats to the floor. No, that isn't real. I swallow. I look at him. Dan. My friend. He looks the same and not at all the same. At the funeral, he collapsed and threw up on my dad's shiny black shoes. His face is tanned. There is a scar that wasn't there before down one cheek. It looks like a crack in marble. He has a small shower of acne on his chin.

"All right," I say. "Okay."

The coffee shop is at the end of the mall, facing out. We don't say anything as we walk. I keep my head low as we pass the store where I stole the shirt. Stole it. I am a thief. My hair masks the writing. In a reflection that we pass, there I am. Hunched and rounded.

The coffee is dark and strong. I don't even drink coffee. I have one cup after another after another. I have to pee like crazy. I light a cigarette. You can smoke in here. It's illegal everywhere, but the girl behind the counter doesn't say anything. I use an empty cup as an ashtray. I spin my lighter on the table.

"So," says Dan. Looking at me. Waiting.

"So," I say.

And then I start to talk. Someone shut me up, please. I can't stop talking. Am I really talking? Words fly out of my mouth and fill the coffee shop. People leave. We are the only people here. I'm talking and talking and talking. I'm not saying the words, they are just there. I have no control.

"Remember when," I say.

"Sam used to," I say.

"I wonder what he'd do," I say. "I wonder what he'd say."

I can't hear myself. The hands on the clock spin round and round. Dan touches my hand.

"I'm so damn tired," I say.

"So am I," he says. "I miss him, too."

He says, "You must think you'll never get over it."

"I won't," I say. And that is the truth. Solid and jagged, like the grey stone of a mountain. A big truth.

He says, "I've missed you, Pagan."

I stop talking. My mouth is dry and aches. I fill it with smoke and blow the smoke out in rings. The girl at the till is tapping her pen on the glass counter. Tap, tap, tap. I reach up and tap my patch. Like she just reminded me. Eventually, she goes around and pulls the metal grille across the front of the shop, leaving it open part way for us to leave.

"Goodnight," she says.

We look at each other and laugh. His front tooth is chipped. It wasn't like that before. I don't remember that. He drives me home in his new truck. I'm shivering cold and I turn on the heat. He doesn't tell me not to. The truck is so new that it reeks of new car smell. It's not a boy's truck. It's a man's truck. It's a truck that you buy after seeing the ad on TV with all the half-naked women and the mud.

"It was a gift," he says. "I hate it."

"Oh," I say. I'm tired of talking. Too tired to ask. I lean back. When he said "gift", something cold and hard moved behind his expression, like a marble rolling past.

"My dad bought it for me," he says. "It's his dream truck."

He handles the vehicle carefully, like he doesn't want to leave a mark on it. Like he doesn't want to care about it. The smell of it is calming. He doesn't play the stereo. I push the cigarette lighter in and wait for it. I pull it out and look into the orange glow. I don't put my finger into it. I don't do that.

"I'm sorry," I say. "For talking so much."

"Chatterbox," he says. "That's okay."

In the driveway, he hugs me good-bye. He smells like a man's cologne. Like a man's sweat. Sam never smelled like that. He smelled like sweat socks and hair gel and onions, usually. My skin jumps where he touches it. I get out of the truck and slam the door. My finger is red and throbbing. It's been a while since anyone has touched me. It's been forever.

I brace myself for confrontation. But when I walk into the kitchen, Mom and Dad barely look up. Mom's face is blotchy. She's been crying. I fight the urge to leave the room, to run up the stairs and hide. I don't want to know, I think. Don't tell me.

"That was Dan," I say. "We had coffee."

Dad says, "Dan. I haven't seen Dan since he puked on my shoes last year. I mean, the year before. Well," he pauses. "You know what I mean."

"Whatever," I say.

"Is he the one that barfed at the funeral?" Mom says.

"Oh God, what a thing to remember." Her eyes fill up again. I hate seeing her grief. I'd rather see her naked. I'd rather see her having sex. Anything.

"I left a message," I say. "I'm sorry I'm late."

"There wasn't a message," Dad says sharply.

"I left one," I lie again. I can almost remember doing it, that's how good a liar I've become. I can imagine myself dialing the number, waiting for the beep.

"I'd ground you, if you ever went out," he says. "I don't know what to do with you."

"Nothing," I say. I shift back and forth from foot to foot. Mom looks at me. She has a carton of milk in her hand, which she puts in the cupboard. She shakes her head and takes it out again and puts it in the fridge. She picks up a plate and puts it down again. Right on the edge of the sink. I watch it to see if it's going to fall.

"Pagan," she says. "Your father and I …"

"Don't," says Dad. He looks tired. He pushes his hair off his forehead. His eyes are red.

Oh, God, I think. Not this. No, no. Not now.

"Listen," I say, "I really have to pee. Can this wait?" Can it wait forever? I add silently.

"She can't handle it," Dad says quietly. As though I can't hear him. As though I'm too fragile to hear it.

"I can handle it, Dad," I say, landing heavily on the Dad. "I think I can handle it."

"There's nothing to handle," he says.

"I was just going to say …" Mom says.

"I really have to use the bathroom," I interrupt. I walk out of the room and up the stairs. My legs are heavy. Dad's right. I can't handle it. I don't want to hear it. What is she going to say? That Dad is having an

affair? What does that have to do with me? He can
screw whoever he wants. It's out of my hands. I'm just
a kid. I don't want to know about their adult problems.

I just hope they don't split up. Our family fractured
at the foot of a snow-covered cliff. Our family floating
apart in the blue of a mountain lake. Screw it, I think.

After I finally pee, I go into my room and flop down
on the bed. It isn't made. I never make my bed anymore. I used to. I used to make Sam's bed, too. He
couldn't be bothered. I made it up tight, with hospital
corners. Sometimes I'd short-sheet his, just for fun. Just
to hear him shout through the wall, "I'm gonna kill
you, P."

On the floor, I find my pillow and hug it to my belly.
I'm light-headed from all the coffee and all the talking.
I am not here. Disoriented. I am somewhere else, watching me lying on the bed. Get up, I think. Get on with it.
I don't move. I'm a character in a movie that I never
signed on for. I'm not in control of my part. I lie here
for a while, fully dressed, and I think about what would
happen if my parents split up. Where would I go? Who
would I go with? Who would get custody of Sam's goddamn ghost? Who gets the grief? Somewhere along the
line, I start crying again. I'm always crying. I don't know
where it all comes from. My pillow is always wet with
it, my lake of tears. I cry and cry and cry and cry until
I fall into one of those dreamless sleeps that leaps out
of the darkness and comes and gets you and pulls you
down into it so deep that you think you might never
wake up.

At least, you hope that you don't.

CHAPTER 3

Did Alice fall down the rabbit hole before or after she swallowed whatever was in that bottle? I can't remember. Or was it cake?

I am Alice. I always feel like Alice in the presence of pills. Eat me, drink me. Grow and shrink. I tell that to Dr. Killjoy. I say, "Alice in Wonderland."

He says, "You aren't the first to say that."

"No one is original," I say.

"That isn't true," he says. "Don't you think you are unique?"

I think of the Prozac dog.

"No," I say. "I think I'm the same as everyone else."

"You aren't," he says. "That I can say for absolute certainty."

"I will be after I take the pill, though, right?" I ask.

"No, Pagan," he says. "You'll still be you. You don't have to take it if you don't want to."

"I want to," I say. I stroke the arm of the chair. It's leather. I wonder how many other people have sat here in this chair, taken this prescription, this neatly written recipe for happiness. I wonder how many of them have left and never come back.

"It's a big decision," he says. "But not the biggest you'll ever make. It's not like choosing a college. It's not like deciding to get married."

"I guess not," I say.

"You can stop taking it if it makes you sick," he says. "If it doesn't help you, we can try something else."

"We," I mimic. "We can always try something else."

"People take this every day," he says. "Millions of people. It will make you feel better. It won't make you grow another head."

"Ha ha," I say. "Millions of crazy people."

"You'd be surprised," he says.

"Do you take it?" I ask.

He stares at me. His eyes don't waver behind his glasses. He doesn't blink. I'm not allowed to ask about him, about his personal life. It's one of the rules. To stop me from falling in love with him, to stop "transference." Psychiatrists talk about transference constantly. It's like they want everyone to love them. There is no one I love less in this world than Dr. Killjoy. He has flakes of dandruff on the shoulders of his black cashmere sweater. The fact he has a black cashmere sweater makes me hate him. It's so obvious. I wait for him to answer. He drops his pen, picks it up and scratches his cheek with it. The ink end. This is how I know.

The whole world is screwed up, I think. I don't get to be an exception.

I go to the drug store. It's one of those places with the prescription pick-up in the back and then aisles of other stuff you have to get through to get out. You can buy a toaster, a computer, a TV, some deodorant and kitty litter. You can buy anything here. They probably have clothes. I don't know. I haven't looked. The piece of paper rustles in my pocket with each step. I don't look at the crap in the aisles. I head straight to the back, with purpose. A normal person doing a normal thing. The lights are too bright in here. They make me nauseated. I stand in line and examine the tiles on the floor. I can't disappear because I'm wearing my patch. I can see people looking at it. People are so rude. I glare at them with my good eye. I figured that in a drug store, I might get away with it. It could be an eye infection, say, not just a weirdness.

In front of me there is a guy. He looks around twenty. Cute. Nice eyes. A skinny nose that curves over at the end like a beak. He bobs up and down, rocking back and forth on his feet. He looks anxious. No, not anxious. Restless. I think he is flirting with me. He keeps looking at me sideways and grinning to himself, like he knows that I know that he notices me noticing him. I turn my patch towards him. Sexy enough for you? I want to say. But I don't. He keeps looking. Smiling.

I smile back. A bit, not a lot. I pull the piece of paper out of my pocket and fold it and refold it. I make the creases sharp with my nails. I keep my eye on him. Touch the patch, just to make sure. Touch it three times. Third time is the charm.

"Come here often?" he says. He twinkles. There is something around his eyes that lets me know that he's kidding. "Uh, what's your sign?"

"Fuck off," I say. But I say it nicely.

"Nice patch," he says.

"It's just plain," I say. I don't know why I say that.

As though I have a bunch of fancier patches at home, I guess. Silk and lace. It was just a stupid thing to say.

"Nothing wrong with plain," he says. "It's, uh, sophisticated."

He scratches his chest. His shirt is missing a button. There is a ketchup stain over his heart. His fingers brush past it.

"Right," I say. "Sophisticated. That's what I was going for." He looks at me. I look at him. Is this what people do? Look at each other, look for each other, look and look and look. He shuffles his feet. Think of something to say, I tell myself. Anything. I look at my watch instead. He looks away. I grin at the back of his head. Too late, too late. What am I doing? I can't do this. I fold the paper into an airplane.

His turn. He gets his pills. Lots of pills, a whole bag full of tiny bottles and instructions. I wonder what is wrong with him. Is he sick? Cancer? AIDS? I feel close to him. A fellow junkie, a pill popper, a swallower of lies. Of knives. I crumple the prescription into a ball. The pharmacist says, "Say hello to your grandma."

"She's out of it," the boy says. "She won't remember you."

"I'm sorry," the pharmacist says.

"Don't be," the boy shrugs. "Cycle of life. At least she's happy."

Happy. I'm jealous. That's how messed up I am. I smooth out the paper against the leg of my jeans. It's barely readable. The ink is cracked from all the folding. Walking by me, the boy shakes his bag of happy pills.

"Well, bye then," he says.

I close my eye, shut him out. What does he want? For

me to say, "Wait, I'll come with you"?

I don't know what normal people do. I tap my patch with the rolled up paper. The pharmacist is looking at me. His eyes are tired, hidden behind trifocals. Everyone is tired. I give it to him. The holy fucking grail, it feels like. Something like that. The pills drop into the bottle all at once, a flock of tiny green birds pushed along by his stick. They rattle and sing. Crazy, crazy, I think. I avoid his eye, magnified behind his weird lenses. I tuck the pills into my backpack.

"Thank you," I say. I pay with change. A pile of quarters, nickels, dimes. It takes a while to count it out.

After that, I walk around the store. I try to stay calm. Flip through a magazine. The lights reflect off the models' white teeth, white eyes, white skin. I decide to buy it. I choose some gum. Tampax. These I don't need. Not now. Not for ages. I have a hundred boxes at home in my closet. I buy them and buy them and buy them and wait for the bleeding to begin. No, sometimes I steal them, but it's the same thing. All in preparation for when my body remembers I've grown up. I'm not a kid anymore. My body is frozen in time, still fourteen and hanging from a rope over a precipice. I had my first period right before Sam died, and then I dried up inside and stopped. I rub my belly. Bleed already, I think. Let's get this thing going again.

I draw red lines on my hand with a lipstick that can't be kissed off. "Wow," I say. "Neat. How useful." I've never kissed a boy. I'm too young for lipstick, too young to kissed. Too old not to have been. I put it back. I don't buy that.

The pills fly around my knapsack all the way home.

I take the bus because I want to hurry. Walking would take an hour. The bus makes me nervous. It's hard to breathe. There is no air. It is too crowded to sit. I have to stand and my legs are rubber and won't hold me. I prop myself up with a pole. Stand next to an open window. Cool air to keep me alive. Inhale, exhale, I think. In and out. People want me to close the window, it's too cold. I shrug and say I can't. It's a lie. It's true. They can suffer. Screw them. It's their fault, anyway, all these people taking up all the stale air. No one presses the issue. No one makes me close it. If someone was really mad, I'd give in. I hate confrontations. I'm a house of cards. I topple easily. I breathe in my victory and shiver. The cold air pushes my hair around. It flicks against people, touches them lewdly in places that it shouldn't. Sticks to them like cobwebs. I don't care and they don't complain. Maybe they like it. Dirty old men. People are standing back and leaving me to stand there in a hurricane of my own hair. They give me the treatment usually reserved for retarded people, handicapped people. Scary people, real people. Crazy people. Every once in a while I move my pack, just to hear the pills calling me. (Swallow me! Eat me!)

I'm scared. It's stupid, but I am.

The house is empty. All this dusty air is mine. I walk from room to room, looking. Mom and Dad's room is tidy as hell. You could bounce quarters on their bed. I sit on it for a minute. I walk down the hall to Sam's room. It's still the same as the day he died. The bed is the only thing that's different. I stripped it, so I could swipe his sheets. There's a pair of dirty socks on the floor. I pick them up and hold them. They are stiff with age. This is disgusting, I think. What kind of shrine is this? I go into the bathroom and wash my hands. I wander through the living room, the dining room, the kitchen. I go into the basement and brush the cobwebs aside with my hand to see our old guinea pig cages. I'm looking for something. I go into the music room and play chopsticks on the piano. This house is empty all the time. Mom and Dad are always at work. This can't be true, I know it can't, but it feels true. Maybe it's just that the house is never filled up. We three are not enough to fill it. It grows every year and we shrink and shrink. We use less of it. The attic, the basement, Sam's room, the den. Unused. Empty.

I go into the kitchen and take one pill out of the bottle and flip it over and over again in my hand until it is sticky with my sweat. It is pale green and yellow. Soft colours. Easter colours. Sam and I had these little things when we were kids, Mexican Jumping Beans we called them. Maybe that's really what they were called, I don't know. Anyway, they were exactly the size and shape of these little pill capsules, but they had faces painted on the end. Eyes. They came in all kinds of colours. Inside them, they had some kind of magnetic ball bearings, polarized so that when you put a bunch together in your hand, they sort of jumped around. They probably don't make them anymore. I would imagine that kids swallowed them. Kids probably died doing that. They were probably full of lead. Sam cut one open once, and we played with the ball bearing from the middle. We rolled it on the fridge and it stuck there. This pill is light and not hollow. I pop it open, wasting it. I inspect its powdery interior. It looks like nothing. I blow the powder off the table and it floats up in a cloud and scatters on the floor. Mixes with the dust. You can't even see it there.

I pour a glass of milk and put it in front of me. The curtains rise and fall in the breeze. I blow milk bubbles for a while, just to make some noise. To hear something. I put a fresh pill beside the milk and look at it. I have an urge to call someone, anyone, and tell them what I'm doing. I don't know who to call. Who would care? Is Dan my friend now? Acquaintance? I don't have friends. "In order to have a friend, you have to be one," Mom says. "Fuck you, Mom," I say out loud. "I have friends." I have school friends. Someone to talk to in class. I eat lunch with this one girl every day. Her name is Brett. She's new at school this year. She's just someone to eat with, though. She isn't a friend. There is a huge difference between someone you share notes with in Algebra and someone who you can call and say, "Help, I'm freaking out here."

"I'm not scared," I say to the pill. Why would I be? I'm a pill swallower. I've swallowed a million, billion pills. There was a time when I would have swallowed every pill in this bottle just to see what would happen, to test the rope that keeps me alive. I stare at the half-drunk glass of white milk. Sam loved strawberry Quick. Sam is in my milk, grinning. Sticking out his tongue. I go get the pink powder and stir it in. Stir him up until the milk is thick with sugar. Now I can't drink it. I gag on the first swallow. This is turning into a huge production, I think. Just take it already.

I dump the milk into the sink and grab a can of Coke instead. I pour it into a glass. I hate the taste of metal. Okay, I say to myself. Just take the pill already, this goddamn miracle pill that they advertise on prime-time TV and write about in fashion magazines. Everyone does it. More people take this than Vitamin C probably. I don't know. If everyone jumped off a cliff, would you?

Yes.

"Okay Sam," I say. "Here goes nothing."

I drink the rest of the Coke slowly. The bubbles burn my throat and turn the pill into acid. My palms sweat, slipping on the glass. Nothing is happening and then nothing and more nothing. The soda bubbles churn in my stomach, turning Prozac into air into bubbles into me.

I want it to make me sleepy. I want it to make me high. I want it to keep me awake forever. I want it to bring back Sam, five feet tall with freckles like constellations on his angel skin. I'm so scared it will take him away instead. I'm scared it will blot him out.

I wait and wait. I sit in the chair and inspect the dregs of my Coke in the light. Dark brown sugar water with rising bubbles, escaping gas. I trace the wood-grain on the table with my finger, trace the fine scars on my hands, trace the keloids on my wrists. The tabletop is cool and smooth. I brush away the morning's toast crumbs and put my cheek down on it and rest. Close my eyes. I take my patch off and rest it on the table, spin it around with my thumb.

A key in the door, footsteps in the hall, shoes being flung into a closet.

"Pagan, what are you doing, honey?" Mom says.

Shut up, Mom, I want to say.

"Waiting," I say. I sit up. Nothing is different. I am talking to my mom through the same old cotton padding. The feathers are in my throat, choking me.

"What are you doing?" she says again.

"Homework," I mumble.

"Where are your books?"

"I …"

"Pagan, you can't do homework without books." Irritation spikes through her voice. Pa-gan. She's pissed. I don't blame her. I am a very irritating person to be around.

"I was thinking about homework," I say. "I was thinking about what I have to do."

"You have to keep up with your school work," she says. "That's all you have to do." She softens, probably remembering advice from her group. You catch more bees with honey, or some other garbage like that. "I'm worried about you," she says. "That's all."

"Whatever," I say. "You don't have to worry about me." I bounce on the balls of my feet so she can see that I am cheerful and not wallowing in self-pity. She hates it when I wallow. Wallow, swallow. I should tell her about the Prozac, but I don't. I go into my room and slam the door. I lie down on my bed. I am always lying here. I wait for the pill to work. I wait for Sam. I wait for a sign. I pull out my books and stare at my homework assignment. It looks so trivial. Who even cares about this stuff? Literature and painting and history. It's all bullshit. It's all something we fool around with to fill the time between being born and being dead. Some of us just have more time to fill, that's all. I answer the questions. They make it easy for us. The answers are all in the books, we just have to parrot them back. I answer them all and then it is done and I lie back and wait some more.

When Mom calls me for dinner, I pretend to be asleep. I hear her say, "She's sleeping, maybe she's coming down with something."

"She's not coming down with something," Dad says. "She's depressed. Wake her up."

"No," Mom says. "She needs her sleep. She's a growing girl."

"She's shrinking," Dad says. "She hasn't grown for a year. She's starving herself to death."

Yay for noticing, I think. Points for you.

"Let her sleep," Mom says. "She's just tired."

"Fine," says Dad. "Whatever you think." I listen for a while to the sound of dishes clinking. I'm not hungry. Darkness spills in through the open window and onto my bed in long, straight shadows. The sky is navy blue and the moon is draped with a funeral veil of clouds. I stare at the moon until the wind sweeps it clean. I look away and see spots.

The phone rings. I let it ring. I know it's for me. I balance the cordless handset on my knee until Mom yells, "Pagan, it's for you!"

"Dan," I say. I know it's him. Call display. I'm not psychic or anything. He's crying on the other end. I let him cry. I play with the phone, listening. Breathing, so he knows I'm here. Here's something I didn't mention before, but should have: Dan is gay. His problems are so much bigger than mine, or so he thinks. I think he thinks so. He is wrong. He has no idea.

I'm not a good friend to him.

The point is, he's crying because he is determined to tell his father. He has the whole scene envisioned, like something from a play. Complete with dramatic exits.

His father will punch him until he bleeds and bruises. His father will throw him out. His father is violent, cruel and sharp-toothed and broad. He is a human Rottweiler, but not trainable like the dog. He's a man who could use some Prozac.

"He's an asshole," I say. "Don't tell him. Why rock the boat?"

"I can't keep it a secret," he says. "He deserves to know."

"If you have to do it, then do it," I say.

"I'm going to," he says. "Should I wait until he's had a drink?"

"You should wait forever," I say. But I cover the mouthpiece so he doesn't hear me. "Whatever you think," I say. "Call me after."

"I'm not going to do it tonight," he says.

Life is all barter and trade. Dan will make a trade with God, maybe, to make his dad accept him. It won't work. There is no God for that. God is too busy taking all the good people while they are young. It must keep Him really occupied. Having a friend is hard work. I don't know how to say the right thing. I don't know what the right thing is to say. While I listen to Dan, I watch the neighbour carrying out his trash. He kicks it when he gets to the curb. He does this every time. I keep listening and I push the window open and climb out onto the sloped roof. "Yes," I say into the phone. "I know he is." I light a cigarette and pull its fire deeply into my lungs. I blow it out in a stream of whiteness. "Who me? I'm fine," I say. I press the burning butt into the bottom of my bare foot. I watch the fire go out. "Nothing is new," I say. I lie back on the shakes and dangle my foot over the drainpipe, waiting for the pain to stop. "See you tomorrow," I say.

I don't tell him about the pill, even though I could. It's my secret, my new secret, wrapped up tight inside me with a green and yellow bow. I hang up the phone. I'm so tired I can hardly keep my eyes open. When will the pill start to work? Nothing is happening. I have Dr. K's answering service on speed dial. I leave a message. "It's not working," I say. "That's the message."

I like to be right. I like to prove people wrong.

I fall asleep on the roof and dream that my mother comes in and tucks me in. I can feel her touching my face gently like she did when I was a little kid. Her hand is cool and soft. I can feel tears start slipping out from under my eyes, but I don't know if she notices or not. She doesn't say anything. Her heels clip-clop on the floor as she walks away. I startle awake in time to see the long tail of a squirrel disappearing down the drainpipe. I look at the ground and think how easily I could have slipped. How quietly I would have landed, caught by the uncut grass and the cradle of the night.

CHAPTER 4

Every day I take a pill. Morning and night. Swallowing and swallowing. Every morning, I get out of bed and flex all my muscles to see if I feel different, but I don't. Nothing has changed. Sam is still gone. I look in the mirror and remember who I am. I skip the shower. My hair falls limp and oily to my hips.

I go to practice. Swimming, volleyball, swimming. Today is swimming, I think. I can't remember. I stand naked in front of the mirror and pull on my suit. It's baggy. My hip bones jut out like small mistakes. When I stand sideways, I disappear. I pull a shirt over my suit and a pair of jeans. Stuff some underwear into my bag with a towel.

I go downstairs. Today is a strange day. The sky is dark and hollow, a storm hiding behind the clouds. Mom and Dad are in the kitchen. Stranger and stranger. I nod at them, hello. Good morning. Whatever. I crack my face in some semblance of a smile. Why are they here? What do they want?

In my pocket, the vial of pills rattles.

"Swim practice today?" Mom asks.

"Yes," I say.

"She's grouchy in the morning," Dad says.

"No, I'm not," I say. "I'm just used to being alone. I don't like to talk." I pour myself a cup of coffee and take it over to the sink. I put my hand in my pocket and try to work the lid off the bottle without taking it out.

"Dad's coming to group with me tonight," Mom says.

"Great," I say. That's screwed up, I think. Now they can gang up on me and say useful things like, "A rolling stone gathers no moss." Crap like that. The lid loosens in my fingers. I work a pill out of the bottle. A bunch of them spill into my pocket. Mom and Dad stare at me. I go take an apple out of the basket and run it under the water. I polish it off and start to eat it, slowly, staring out the window.

"You should eat more than that, shouldn't you?" Mom says. "Your body needs fuel to perform."

"I'll eat later," I say. "After."

"How *is* swimming?" Dad asks.

"Fine," I say. I think of how the blue water stings my eyes, slows my stroke, tries to pull me under. How it calls to me. "It's good," I say. I don't tell him that I'm about to be cut from the team because I can't make my usual times. I don't tell him that every time I pull my arm back and over my head to pull myself through the water, it's like moving a thousand pound weight.

"When's your first meet?" he says. "I'd like to come."

"Give me a break," I say.

"Don't be rude," Mom says.

I twist the pill around in my fingers. Put my head down. Pop it into my mouth and under my tongue. I take a gulp of coffee and scald my tongue. The first meet is next week. I'm not in it. I'm not on my form. I asked to be left out.

"Back injury," I told my coach. He didn't believe me. He spat when he talked. "Pull yourself together, Pagan," he said. If he knew how many people had said that to me for how many years. "I'm trying," I told him. "Give me one more chance." *Let him cut me*, I was thinking. *Let him cut me loose.*

The pill is stuck in my mouth. I can't swallow it. The coffee is too hot. The pill dissolves and fills me up with bitterness. I go to the cupboard and take out some Vitamin C and make a big show of taking one with a glass of juice. I gulp the cold drink quickly. I rinse it around to rid myself of the taste. I take a multi-vitamin, too. To make a point. The pills in my stomach knock together. The rattle on the tail of a snake. I rub my belly.

"I'm going to be late," I say. Just to say something.

"There might be scouts from colleges at the meets this year, Pagan," Mom says to my back.

I turn around. "I'm not going to college, Mom," I say. "I haven't decided what I'm going to do yet."

The kitchen is cold and silent. They stare at me. *What?* I want to say. *What do you want from me?* Dad is in his pajamas. There is a hole under one of his arms, frayed around the edges.

"Of course you're going to college," he says. He blows on his coffee and then slurps it back with a toss of his head. "All the Riddlers go to college."

"Not all of them," I say. The door behind me is open. "Sam didn't." I let the door swing shut, softly. Run down the front walk, left right left right. Inhale, exhale. College. Swim meets. Why do they suddenly care? It's like after three years of tiptoeing around, waiting for me to die or implode, they've suddenly decided that I'm going to live. That I should get on with it. Well, they can go screw themselves. What do they know about me?

I have to run to get the bus. I can hear it behind me, sighing as it rounds the sharp corner. My heart is racing. I've been taking this pill for days. Nothing is happening, still. Nothing. I still have to remind myself to breathe. The sidewalk still calls to me, I could fall at any moment. I feel nothing. I feel grief. Still and still and still and always.

On the bus, I fall asleep, my head against the steamed window. I wake up tasting bile and realize I've gone past my stop. I have to run back. My feet hammering on the sidewalk. I feel like I'm not running, like I'm only remembering running.

I am late. I wasn't lying when I said I would be. This will be the third time this year. Coach won't put up with that for long. He sees me and gestures with his hand. The gesture could mean anything. Cut me, I think. Asshole. Cut me from this team. I don't care. I throw my outer layer of clothes on the floor of the change room, pass through the shower just to get wet, walk as fast as I can across the pool deck before falling into the water's cool embrace.

I only liked swimming when I went with Sam. We used to race each other to the pool on our bikes. We used to race each other into the pool. He would always be in the water first — a faster changer, I guess. He was better at butterfly, a stroke I could never quite grasp. But I could lap him doing the crawl, front and back. I was better. On the weekends, we would go to the pool and race in the morning. Race through the day. I swim a slow lap and swallow mouthfuls of chlorine, mouthfuls of Sam.

Left, right, left, right, inhale. That's how I swim my

laps. Left, right, left, right, inhale. I'm a machine. From far away, I hear Coach's whistle. I keep swimming, one arm and the other. Kicking. I get out only once to get the buckets to tie to my feet, to slow me down. One lap, two laps, fifty laps, a hundred.

I'm sick. My stomach is upset. I pull myself out of the pool on rubber arms and go to the shower, get dressed. The smell of chlorine is making me gag. Coach is waiting for me outside, but I ignore him. Stare at him balefully through my one good eye. He's scared to yell at me. I'm damaged goods. He doesn't want to be the one to push me over the edge. No one does. If no one ever pushes me, I think, I'll dangle here forever.

I want to fall. I want to die. This pill isn't working, and it was my last hope. My only hope. If I die, I get to be with Sam. I keep thinking that. It's an idea I can't get out of my head, like a song permanently etched into my brain that I can't stop singing. Sam would think it was stupid, to kill myself. I mean, if I had died, I sure wouldn't have wanted him to go killing himself. At least, that's what Dr. K. tells me, to keep me from trying again. I'm so tired today. It almost seems like a good idea. Sam's dead. He doesn't care about me now. He's dead, dead, dead. Expired, extinguished, extinct. His body is rotting in lake water, trapped in a tangle of weeds, too deep to ever be found.

How can I live with that?

I'm a cat. Nine lives. This is the last one.

I get on the bus to go to school. I watch out the window while it stops and starts and stops and starts. The day is grey still. The storm is beginning to blow. Treetops lean and stretch into the cold air. Early morning dew shines dully on lawns and rooftops.

Sam and I used to love the end of autumn because it meant it was almost winter. Winter meant skiing. Skiing meant everything. Once a week, we got up at four in the morning and rode three buses and a train to get to the mountain. When we were twelve, we got our own skis for Christmas. We waxed them until they gleamed. They flew us down mountains like soaring birds. The air pushed us up. We were weightless. Racing over moguls and flying. The soft cushion of snow under our skis. I remember how it was always sunny, although it couldn't have been. I remember that the sun turned our hair blond and our skin brown, leaving a white mask where our goggles had been. How the muscles in our legs grew strong and round. I remember all of it.

Now this weather means nothing to me. Winter means nothing to me. Snow means nothing to me. Nothing means anything. I blow steam onto the window and write "Sam" with my finger and then smear it with my hand before anyone sees it.

It's when I'm walking from the bus up the sidewalk to the school that all of a sudden I feel different. Not a lot different, a little different. Like when the piano needs tuning and all of a sudden you are aware of a string that vibrates too high, a note that pulls itself slightly off key. Like a prickling in the back of my neck has stopped. Like someone has opened a window and I have just tasted fresher air, just realized the air I was breathing before was flawed. Choking.

It lasts a second, then I gag. I'm sick. Little kid sick.

The kind of sick where you know you are going to throw up and there is nothing you can do about it.

"Pagan!" someone calls.

"Pagan," I repeat. Swallowing bile. Swallowing blood. Swallowing Sam. I turn around slowly.

"What's the matter?" Brett asks. I squint at her. She looks a long way away. Brett, my lunch friend. My new friend. Is she a friend? A galaxy of lights spins around her head and makes me dizzy. Her voice is coming through a tunnel.

"I don't feel good," I say.

I throw up in a bush. Her eyes on me like leeches, staring. I heave and heave. It's so cold that my puke steams. How disgusting. How embarrassing. Kill yourself, I think automatically. You can kill yourself. I am a crazy and embarrassing person. I start to cry, standing there, hunched over. Her hand touches my back. She steers me to a bench.

"Don't help me," I say. "Go away."

"Don't be stupid," she says. "What's wrong with you?"

"Nothing," I say. "I was at swim practice." As though that explains it. The school bell goes. Everyone disappears inside. "You better go," I say. "You'll be late."

"I'll call someone for you," she says. "Who should I call? You should go home."

"I'm okay," I lie. My hands are shaking. I light a cigarette but I can't inhale. The smell makes me gag. I put it out on the ground, grind it in with my foot. "Maybe my dad," I say. "But I'll call, you'll be late."

"I don't give a shit," she says. "I'm calling. Let me help you." She disappears inside. I lean back on the bench and close my eyes. Then she is there again.

"He's coming," she says. She sits there and doesn't say anything. She taps her heel on the ground. She is wearing high-heeled boots, black and shiny. Some kind of plastic. Her feet must sweat in those, I think. They're hideous, but she carries them off. I stare at her foot, tapping.

"Are you in trouble?" she says. "If you are, you know, I can help."

"In trouble?" I repeat. A gull circles low above us and drops a starfish at our feet. She kicks it with her pointed toe. It spins away and skids to a halt against the curb. My dad's car pulls up. His tie is loosened and he looks harassed.

"Thanks," I tell her. "I owe you one."

She shrugs. "Whatever."

In trouble, I think as I slide into the passenger seat and pull the seatbelt tight around me. I'm almost home when I realize what she meant. "In trouble" she said. "Pregnant," she meant. I start to laugh. She doesn't know me at all.

"What's funny?" Dad says.

"Nothing," I tell him. "Nothing at all."

"What's wrong with you?" he says. He means for it to be nice, but it comes out wrong. What's *wrong* with you?

"I'm in trouble," I whisper.

"What?" he says.

"Swallowed too much pool water, I guess," I say. I look out the window and count white houses. One, two, three, four. I tap my patch four times. Compulsive behaviour, Dr. K. would say. Typical symptom.

"You're too good a swimmer to be swallowing water," he says.

"How would you know?" I say. "Besides, no one is too good to swallow water. It's not a skill. It just happens." A white apartment building. Ten apartments, I guess. I don't know for sure. I just tap and tap. Why the hell not? My stomach churns and grumbles.

"Pagan," he says. "You should eat proper breakfasts, then maybe this wouldn't happen."

"Maybe it wouldn't," I say. "Maybe it would." My stomach kicks. I open the window and breathe through the crack.

"You smell like smoke," he says. "Have you been smoking?"

"Yes," I say.

"For Christ sake," he says. "You aren't allowed to smoke."

"Okay," I say. "Fine."

"Okay, fine?" he says. "What is that supposed to mean?"

I gag and dry heave. "Leave me alone," I say. "Just leave me alone for a minute."

"Don't throw up in the car," he says. As though I could get out at this speed, as though I have a choice.

"You know," he says, "I want you to feel like you can talk to me. If you need someone to talk to. You can."

I look over at him and then I see it. He's crazy, too. Crazier than me. He's doing what he thinks he should. He's making Dad sounds, saying Dad things. He isn't my dad. He is an old man in a suit. There is a patch of hair on his chin where he missed with his razor. His hair is thinning. He has aged ten years since Sam. Well.

Who hasn't?

"You pay Dr. K. to listen to me," I say. Hating him. "You don't have to bother."

He winces like I've struck him. I wish I had struck him. I want to slap him. To punch him. To see his head spin around in surprise as my fists rain down on him, my scarred hands pummeling him, hating him. I'll never forgive him, I think, for taking us on that trip to begin with.

"It's your fault," I say. The words are bigger than the car and crush him. I watch him vanish in a streak of blood. "He wouldn't have died if you'd …"

"For Christ sake, Pagan," he says. I get out and slam the door, looking at him.

"Fuck you," I say to the closed window. The tires screech as he pulls away. He doesn't even check to see if I have a key. To see if I can climb back into the empty house. To see if I have a way in.

I don't have a key. I kick the basement window in with my foot. The glass scrapes through my sock and cuts my ankle. I kick it and I kick it and I kick it until the glass is completely gone. It crunches under my feet like ice. I climb in. I get a garbage bag and tape it over the hole. Probably no one will notice. I go upstairs and empty my pocket of Prozac. I throw it in the garberator and turn it on. The gears grind. I add some water and listen to it disappear. In the bathroom, I fill the tub. What am I doing? I think. I'm crazy. I look for a razor, but there isn't one. The water is hot and steaming. I forget that my stomach is upset and I sit on the edge of the tub. I run my fingers through the water. Hold my hand under the water until it turns red from the scalding heat. What am I doing? What am I doing?

I can't do this.

Not again.

I let the water out. The house drinks it back like a thirsty dog. I can hear it swallowing. This house is alive, I think. Everyone in it is dead.

I go into my room and climb back between the sheets. The sheets are cool and safe. Rain starts to fall and flicks against the window. I open my eyes and watch it fall. Rain, snow. Snow makes me think of Sam, makes me think of walking in those stupid snowshoes, our footprints splayed and wide. Makes me remember how he laughed when I ate some snow. I was so thirsty. "Bears have peed there, you know," he said. And laughed and laughed. "Don't fight," Dad said, automatically, and we flipped him the bird behind his back. I think of how the rope pulled when Sam lagged behind.

Groundhog Day. That's what my life is like. A stupid movie. One day lived and relived and relived over and over again. When we saw that movie, Sam said, "I'd kill myself." I remember him saying that. Was that some kind of message to me? Did he know what was coming?

Of course not, I tell myself. Of course he didn't. He didn't know. He wouldn't really.

"Leave me alone," I say. "Sam, would you please leave me alone?" My stomach flip-flops again and I go down to the kitchen for ginger ale. There isn't any. I pour a glass of juice instead. The rain is pouring down outside, I can hear it rushing through the eaves troughs like a river. I think, *I'll go outside. I'll let it wash me clean.*

The phone rings. I'm still standing there, holding the

juice. The ringing of the phone makes me want to drop it, but I don't. I put it down carefully. It's Brett. Brett, I think. Who is Brett? Then I remember. My lunch friend. My saviour.

"Brett," I say.

She must be calling from the foyer of the school. Behind her is the barnyard noise of a thousand students shifting from one classroom to the next.

"I was asking if you were pregnant," she says. "If you are, I know someone who can help. I mean, if you want."

"I'm not pregnant," I say. I twist the phone chord around my arm. Around and around. I stick my finger through the coils. "I don't even have a boyfriend."

"You don't have to have a boyfriend to get pregnant," she says. "Anyway, I just thought if you were …"

"I'm not," I say. "Thanks, though." My voice sounds too loud in the room. It bounces off the floor and echoes. I'm getting a headache. "I guess I'm getting a migraine. You know."

"Oh," she says. "I've never had one." I can hear the bell going behind her, shrill. She has to go.

"I take these pills," I say. "For, um, migraines. They make me sick, you know. Sometimes. I just … Anyway, thanks."

The dial tone hums in my ear. She's already gone. Her question asked and answered. "Okay, then," I say to it. "Good-bye. Thank-you for calling."

I sit down at the table. Am I making friends now? I wonder. The rain explodes off the sidewalk and bounces back up again. The tree in the yard bends low under the weight of the shower. I go stand by the window and look out. As I watch, the rain turns to hail. It smashes against the glass. A car parked across the street vibrates under its assault. I open the door and go stand in it. Why not? It hammers down on me, but I can hardly feel it. It's just weather. It doesn't mean anything. Lightning cracks down and I think, *let it hit me, please let it hit me.* I close my eye, but nothing happens.

Crazy, I think. *Crazy Pagan. Her brother died, you know. She never got over it.*

I go back inside and call my shrink. A normal person would call their Mom, I guess. I call Dr. K.

"Help," I say. "Help me. I can't do this anymore."

I go back to bed and close my eyes. Here it is: is it a dream or is it real? Did I call or didn't I? The line between what I imagine and what I make up fades and vanishes. There is the ambulance again. The emergency room. The psychiatrist. The crazy ward.

Home sweet home, I think. I don't talk. I open my mouth and a flock of birds escapes and flaps around the room, trapped. Dr. Killian visits me. "You can go home as soon as you're ready," he says. "Think of it as a break from everything." He opens the window and the birds disappear into the sunlight.

I stare him down. He leaves. He comes back in the morning. "I'm changing your dose," he says. "It should start to work soon."

My mouth is sewn shut. I lie between the thin sheets and dream of flannel. I listen to the other patients screaming and dream of home. I close my eyes and dream of flying. My pills are delivered in paper cups and I swallow them and think of Jack Nicholson in that movie where the Native guy throws the fridge through the wall. No one here could do that. I could do that if I wanted to, I'll bet. I swallow the pills. I dream of throwing up. I wake up, gagging.

Crazy, I think.

Is this a dream?

I wake up in my own bed at home, not knowing if it happened or not. Outside, the hail pounds the pavement. Was that a dream or did it happen? I go downstairs, I call Dr. K. "Something's wrong," I tell him. "I'm coming in."

I take a cab to his office. "Quite a hailstorm," the cabby says.

"Yes," I say. "Quite a hailstorm."

winter

CHAPTER 5

My dreams are full of water. Dr. Killian tells me the pills are starting to work. I try to believe him. They at least make my dreams colourful. Technicolor. I wake up gasping for air. In my dream, I was drowning. I mention it to Brett. "I have drowning dreams," she says. "I have flying dreams. I dream that my teeth fall out." I mention it to Dan. "I have dreams where I can't move," he says. "I have dreams that the water is full of sharks and I have to swim through."

I have all of those. I am not special. I am not different. And now more than ever my dreams are the same as everyone else's. It's a universal experience, dreaming. We all dream the same. Sam and I used to have the same dreams sometimes, but now I realize there is nothing special about that. It's just a human thing. It's all the same experience.

I don't dream so often about Sam, falling. About the rope giving way.

Prozac gives my dreams sharp sparkling edges, like silver blades.

In my drowning dream, I'm not afraid. I am buoyed up by the water, floating just above it. I am at swim practice. Even in my sleep, I can feel the pull and weight of the water. I can hear the hollow echo of the voices on the pool deck, the shrill demands of Coach's whistle. I stretch and move through the water, but I'm heavy. I'm too heavy. I turn to the side to pull in air and I notice that I'm below the surface. It's too late. I don't care. I sink in slow motion to the bottom of the pool where the stripe is painted in darker blue and then I slide down into the stripe, into something deeper. I let myself fall. I don't bother to try to get up. My dream is heavy and warm and the water brightens and becomes turquoise blue like a mountain lake. I feel happy. I feel at peace. I want to stay here forever, but I know I can't.

That's what Prozac does. It makes me unafraid. But only while I'm sleeping. When I'm awake, the monsters are all the same.

On this particular morning, it's the frozen rain that has woken me up, otherwise I would have been happy to stay in that dream. The small pellets of ice demand my attention. Outside, it is still dark. I open my eyes and close them and can't see the difference. The shadows are the same, open and closed. A rich, velvet of blackness. I like the nights the best. I like to be asleep. I count backwards from a thousand, trying to find the dream again. I imagine that I could have opened my eyes and not been alone. I could have found Sam in that blue water. The rain is loud, like applause. Splattering on the window, hard, like it's demanding that I wake up or just that it wants me to look. Fuck off, I think. The dream wobbles and evaporates. I open my eyes and look around to see if anything is different, like I do every day, like I've done every day since the first time I swallowed a pill. Dr. K. says it takes time to build up in your system, it takes time for the balance of neuro-transmitters to change. It's different for everyone, he says. For some people, it's almost immediate.

I've been taking them for weeks, swallowing them down, choking and gagging, and the only thing that's changed is my dreams. I think maybe I'm immune, maybe this miracle doesn't work on people who are crazy like me. Dr. K. gives me stuff to read about other people and what happened to them, but I don't read it. The paper piles up on my desk and I ignore it. There are whole books on the subject of this one pill. *Prozac Nation*, *Prozac Diary*. Prozac is goddamn everywhere. I feel like the last person in the room to get the joke. I don't care about other people, I just want it to be different for me. I want to have a reason for taking the pills, I want to have a reason to get up.

I get up. Every day. I go to school, I go to practice, I come home. I walk around the empty house, I kick the dust bunnies into corners, I play the piano, play the guitar. I sit at the dinner table and lift food to my mouth. I get through one day and then the other. I don't kill myself.

"You go, girl," I say. "Good for you."

Winter slides towards my world like the backdrop of a Broadway show. Swoops in when I'm not looking. The air bites my cheeks and turns them red. My breath hangs in front of my face in clouds of my own making, mixing in with the smoke I suck in. I'm up to a pack a day. I have to steal them. I can't afford to buy them. I'm becoming someone I don't recognize, slipping farther and farther away from Sam.

Sam wouldn't be a thief. Sam wouldn't steal a pack of cigarettes from the open purse of an old lady who has fallen asleep on the bus, a pack of cigarettes so old that the foil paper inside crumbles to the touch. Why did she even have them? I wonder. An ex-smoker waiting for the next craving to hit? They tasted stale and alive. I smoked them anyway. I have nothing else to do. I perch on benches and rooftops and sidewalks, waiting.

I wait and I wait and I wait.

I watch the neighbour take out the garbage and kick the bags. I sit out on the slippery shakes, shivering, smoking a cigarette before bed.

I see my shrink.

Keep going, I tell myself. I'm working towards something. I'm working towards surviving.

Dan and I are in the coffee shop. Once a week, now, we go there and talk. It's a habit we just slipped into. I don't want to make too big of a deal about it. I don't want to turn it into something it's not, some big friendship or something. It is something. I just don't know how to label it. Just enjoy it, Dr. K. suggests. Everything doesn't have to have a name. We sit hunched over the table and wait for each other to talk.

"Do you think Sam was gay?" I ask him. I'm hoarse. I have a sore throat. From all that smoking, or from the start of a flu. I can't tell. Do I have a fever? My face feels hot.

"What?" he says.

"You guys were friends," I say. I'm blushing. Not a fever.

"Don't be an idiot," he says. "Besides, Sam was too young to be anything." I shrink down to nothing and blow away. What a stupid question. I'm stupid and crazy. Quite a combination. Stop it, I tell myself.

I don't say anything. I gulp down some coffee. Flick a little creamer around with a stir stick. Nothing is changing. Everything is the same.

"I hate Christmas," he says. Explosively. He looks at me. "I fucking hate Christmas."

I love you, I think suddenly. That's what this is. That's why I couldn't name it. Love. Is it? Or is it just familiarity? Familiarity breeds contempt, my mom would say. I look at his familiar face. Brown eyes rimmed with green. Chin acne half hidden by a stubbly goatee. "I hate it, too," I say. "I hate all the Hallmark holidays."

Oh, God, I think. Don't fall for Dan. Don't be stupid. Something in my heart opens and closes hard. A door slamming. He's gay. Gay, gay, gay.

"Do you ever think …?" I start to ask.

"What?" he says.

"Nothing," I say. I let the silence fall back down again. He gets up to get a cup of coffee. The coffee shop is decorated for the season. It's only November. I'm glad I don't work here. I'm glad I don't have to look at these flashing lights all day long, listen to the same old songs.

At the next table, there is a couple. They aren't talking much. He leans over and pushes her hair out of her eyes. My heart thuds. She smiles at him and sips his coffee. Are they dating? Married?

I can't imagine dating anyone. Yes, I can. I can almost imagine dating Dan. People think we're dating. Brett asked me just the other day. "He's hot," she said. "If you're not seeing him, do you mind if I go for it?" Do it, I told her, laughing. I wouldn't tell her why. I wouldn't tell her that the only person Dan is interested in is Steve, captain of the rugby team, boyfriend of some idiotic cheerleader or another. It changes from day to day, Steve's girlfriend. He thinks Dan is his buddy. Poor Dan, I think. Poor me.

"I wish you weren't gay," I mumble when he's out of earshot. He's only seventeen, I think. How does he know for sure? How do I know for sure that I'm not? Maybe I'm gay, too. I don't even know myself well enough to know that. I look up at Dan, standing in line, waiting for his refill. I'm thinking about telling him, confiding in him. I'd rather confide in him than Brett, after all. I feel the need to tell someone. Dr. Killjoy would say that I'm trying to reach out to people, but I don't think that's it. I'm just tired of the secret. Maybe if I tell someone, it will help. What would I say? "Hey, I'm taking Prozac!" What would I say if someone told me that?

Nothing. I wouldn't know what to say.

There is a guy in front of Dan in line. A man. Business suit and a lap-top in a leather shoulder bag. His cell phone rings. "Hello," he yells into it. Everyone is looking at him. "Hello," he yells again. "Piece of crap phone." In between calls, he's ordering a coffee, something long and ridiculous. "Extra caff, run through twice, half-fat, shot of vanilla." One of those guys. The girl behind the counter is flustered. Her cheeks are flushed. She looks at the line-up forming. I can see her start to panic. I recognize the look. The guy is getting impatient. "What's wrong with you?" he sneers. I feel sorry for her, but what am I going to do? He's getting excited. He reaches into his jacket. *Fuck*, I think. *He's going to shoot her.*

For a minute, I'm excited. Maybe he'll shoot us all. I imagine the headline. The pictures in the paper. On the news.

No, that isn't what he does. He pulls out his keys, car keys, a million keys flashing silver in the twinkling lights. "Forget it," he says. "If you can't do it, then forget it." The keys jingle like bells. He shakes them at her, as though it's a threat. She bursts out laughing. It's from fear. Shock. Her laugh is hysterical. The man gives her the finger. "Fucking waste case," he says. "You're a waste of air."

"Man," says Dan. "Take a fucking Prozac."

I freeze. The mouthful of coffee I just swallowed hovers in my throat. Take a fucking Prozac, I think. I start to choke, coffee spilling out of my mouth and onto the table. I cough and cough. My eyes stream red. Dan is behind me, slapping me on the back. Shaking me. I draw in my breath. Sharp. Like I'm drowning.

"I'm okay," I say. "Lay off." He slaps me again.

"Hey," I say. "Don't."

I push him. I push him hard. He wasn't ready for it. His eyes are surprised, round. Stupid. He falls backwards into a chair, the chair skidding under his weight. "Take a fucking Prozac," I hear my voice say. My heels clicking on the floor as I hurry away. Hurry home. Hurry, hurry, hurry.

I escape into my bed again. Mom knocks on the door. "Pagan, are you sick?"

"Yes," I croak. "I'm sick."

"Want me to make you some soup?" she says.

"Yes," I say, giving in to her. "Yes, please."

But I'm asleep before she brings it, and when the alarm goes off in the morning I reach up to turn it off and knock the soup to the floor. Cold and congealed. It takes me a few minutes to notice, to see what I have done. I get up. I clean up the soup. I take a shower. I'm halfway down the stairs when I realize that something *is* different. Something has changed. There is a curious feeling at the base of my neck that is neither good nor bad, just present. I feel like I move more easily through the air in the house. I feel not like myself.

I go back into the bathroom and look in the mirror. Looking for something. Looking for a sign. The mirror is steamed up. "Pagan," I say to my blurred reflection. It sounds normal-ish. As normal as you can sound when you are talking to yourself in the mirror.

Oh my God, I think. It's working. It's starting to work. I go back into my room and dial Dr. K.'s machine. "I think it's working," I say. "It's working."

It's that simple. It is. Like a switch flicking. Or like a scale sliding into balance. I feel better, I hum to myself. I feel better.

It's a fucking miracle. To Dr. K.'s machine I say, "I feel cautiously optimistic." I hang up. I wait for the feathers to move into my throat and choke me. I wait to feel angry.

I feel nothing.

It's early. I go to the piano. It's been a long time since I did that before breakfast, although I do play some every day. I play carefully, like the piano might break or float away. It sounds a little better than usual, better than yesterday. Something is definitely changing inside me, and I feel a little bit afraid, a little bit out of control, a little bit giddy.

I play something new, and it doesn't sound all jagged and rough and sloppy. It sounds pretty good. I play something old, something Sam and I made up when we were younger. It's sort of a rip-off of an Elvis Presley song. I play that, pounding down hard on the black keys and sliding off the white keys like it's a dance that my fingers are doing. I probably woke up Mom and Dad, but I don't care. I play and I play and I start to feel that familiar sadness again. Which, in a weird way, makes me feel better. So I stop.

At breakfast, I drink my usual orange juice, but then I feel hungry. Like there is a void inside me that an apple couldn't fill. I boil the kettle and make a bowl of instant porridge. The steam smells delicious, hot and spiced with cinnamon. "I feel different," I want to tell someone. Because I do.

I look at Mom and Dad, but they look annoyed. Mom doesn't like to be woken up before her alarm goes off. They mumble to each other, "Pass the cream," "Do you want more toast," that kind of thing. Nothing meaningful. I don't say anything, I stare down into the oatmeal and breathe in all the hot spicy smell of it.

I feel pretty good.

I don't feel like throwing up.

"What's on your schedule today?" Dad asks.

"I thought I'd go to school," I say, grinning, so he knows I'm being cheeky, not rude. "You?"

"Oh, I thought I'd go to work," he says.

Mom doesn't say anything, but she's looking at me strangely. She is eating a soft-boiled egg, like she does every day. My mom is big into routine. She eats exactly one bite of toast and then one bite of egg, and she knows exactly how big or small these bites have to be so that she runs out of egg and toast at the same time. Obsessive-compulsive, Dr. K. might say. Not uncommon in people with depression. People like me, he meant. I don't have that, though. I don't wash my hands a hundred times a day or count my steps. The only thing I count is my pulse and that's just because I'm checking to see if I'm still alive. I feel my wrist under the table, automatically counting. It's steady and strong.

I tap my patch. Just once. I don't go crazy.

"What about you, Mom?" I say, to include her.

"Work," she says. "Pagan, I go to work every day."

"Just making conversation," I say.

"Have you thought about working yourself?" she says.

"What?" I say. "What are you talking about?"

"Well," she says, "if you aren't going to college, you should think about looking for a job."

"Oh," I say. "Well, I might go to college. I just don't know yet." Upstairs in my room, I have a pile of applications. We all got them. They gave them to us in homeroom. I meant to throw them out, but then I kept them. Stuffed them in a drawer. I haven't looked at them since. Haven't thought about them. Not much, anyway.

"Well, you should decide soon, kiddo," Dad says.

"I know," I say. "I'm just not sure."

My mom finishes her egg, stands up and brushes the crumbs off her suit. "We'll be late tonight," she says.

"It's group night."

"Right," says Dad. "Will you be okay, Pagan? Or do you want to come?"

"Uh, no thanks," I say. "I'm sure I'll be fine." It's not like I've ever not been fine when they go to group. I just usually eat a frozen diet dinner in front of the TV. It's not like we're the Cleavers and we all eat together and compare notes about our day. It's not like Mom whips up a big roast beef dinner on a nightly basis.

I got up so early that even with breakfast done with and the dishes put away so Mom doesn't freak out, I don't have to rush to school. I walk slowly up the street and look at the neighbours scraping frost from their windshields and I let the icy drizzle sting my skin. I step on a leaf and feel it crumble under my foot.

I think about Dan. I'm still mad. He doesn't even know why. Well, I don't care. I think about Brett and think that maybe today I'll ask her if I can come with her to one of her parties. I think it's weird that I stay home every weekend and do nothing, except sometimes play games with my parents. Stupid games, like Monopoly and Scrabble. Games we all used to play together. I think Brett probably thinks it's weird. Maybe she's scared to ask me. We've only known each other for a couple of months, and I've been kind of weird in that time. She doesn't have that many other friends at school, though. Her friends are older. She eats lunch with me every day.

I'm going to ask her, I decide. Why not? She scares me a little bit, I admit to myself. She's so beautiful and wild, not like me. She isn't quiet, that's for sure. She doesn't read. She sure doesn't play games with her parents on Saturday nights.

I make it through the morning without falling asleep, which is impressive for me. Usually I doze off at least once by third period. I'm not that interested in my classes, but I try to pay attention. What if I do want to go to college after all? I have to get good grades, I guess. Just in case.

At lunch, I go to a special volleyball practice and actually make a suggestion about the uniforms. I mean, I don't really care about them, but I think we should get new ones. A lot of people agree with me. It feels strange to be the centre of attention. It feels okay. I think people are surprised. I hardly ever say anything at practice, but I play really hard. I know they only keep me on the team because I'm good. Coach has told me more than once about "team spirit" and blah blah blah. But he can't cut me, because I'm the best player.

After practice, I try to find Brett, but I can't. I didn't see her in class this morning, but she's only in one of my classes and she doesn't sit near me. Sometimes she's there and I don't notice. But today, I can't find her anywhere. I wait by her locker for a while and then I start to feel self-conscious, being alone with no one to talk to, while everyone else runs around in groups of two or three, laughing and talking. My old friends Trina and Ashley pass me and they don't even look at me. I guess I don't blame them. I was pretty mean to them for, well, for the last three years almost I guess. I slide down the lockers and sit on the floor and pretend to read for a while, and then I give up and go out into the breezeway and have a cigarette. I don't usually smoke a lot. I do, but I didn't use to. Now I smoke like I can't stop. Like smoke is my source of oxygen. It's stupid, but it somehow makes it easier to breathe. I don't want to live forever anyway. Obviously. I like smokers. They never question why you are there. It's obvious. You're smoking. That's the only place to do it. It's a secret club. The only club I belong to.

"Gotta lighter?" some kid asks, his face really close to mine, and I almost jump out of my skin.

"Jumpy, aren't you?" he says and laughs.

I laugh, too, to be polite and give him my lighter. It's just one of those disposable ones. I feel kind of nervous after that so I go inside. I forget to get it back, but I don't much care. He can keep it.

At home, I try thinking about Sam, on purpose, and I get sad, but I don't have to leave the room crying. I just feel sad in a sort of normal way. I don't want to tell anyone, but I'm bursting to tell someone. I call Dr. K.'s office and listen to his voice unwind slowly on his answering machine. "I'm currently with a client. Please leave a message, and I will call you back when I'm free. If this is an emergency, please call blah, blah, blah." I breathe into the phone, but I don't say anything. When the machine starts beeping like crazy, I hang up and go back to the music room. I don't play, I just sit there quietly at the piano, thinking. Waiting, I guess. Waiting for something to go wrong.

It doesn't.

I cut my finger with a kitchen knife. On purpose. I watch as it bleeds. It doesn't even hurt the same way. I don't even remember why I did it, as soon as the blade touches my skin. I feel stupid. I wrap it in a Band-Aid so no one will see.

A couple of days later, it's finally my appointment day with Dr. K. After school, I fly to Dr. Killjoy's office. I swear my feet aren't touching the ground. I'm no longer pretending to myself that this is just a fluky good mood. It's like breathing after holding your breath for a hundred years. I stand on the bus like a normal person, and unless I put my finger on my wrist, I am not aware of my own heart thundering in my ears. I even smile at the driver when I get off.

I say, "Have a nice day."

I said that. It felt real.

I go into the waiting room and wait for my turn and I admire the paintings on the wall. I ask the receptionist if they are new and she says, "No, Pagan, they are the same as they always were."

"Oh," I say. "I guess they are."

It's the pill, I tell myself. It isn't real, this feeling that things are new, that things are different. Nothing is different. It just all looks different, tastes different, smells different. It's different enough for me.

Dr. Killjoy is sitting behind his desk as usual and looking out the window into the rain that slaps lightly against the glass and streaks downwards like tears.

"Depressing weather," he says and sighs. "How are we today?"

"Must be good for business," I tease him. That's not me. I don't usually tease people. At least, not recently. I sit down. I press down on my patch with the heel of my hand. My eye itches underneath. I flip it up and rub for a minute. "We're fine," I add. "Why do you say 'we' when you mean me?"

He looks at me quizzically. "How are *you* feeling?"

"I feel pretty good," I tell him, grinning like crazy. "I feel good! Maybe you were right about this pill. I think you were right. It's crazy. I feel good. Good crazy, not bad crazy. I feel good." I want to keep saying it over and over.

"Hmm," he says and leans back in his chair. He puts his hands behind his head and stares at me for a couple of minutes. "So, it's started working, has it?" he says. "Remember, don't expect too much from it. It's a pill, not a miracle." He tells me all about how the drug works and I half-listen, but I don't really care. Serotonin inhibitors or whatever don't interest me that much. He talks and talks and then the session is over and I jump up because I can't wait to get out of there. I feel like there is something I need to do, or some place I need to be. Or maybe I just want to go home.

"I think it is a miracle, Dr. Killian," I tell him on my way out the door. "It is for me."

CHAPTER 6

In behind the house, there is a garden shed. There's a bunch of junk in it. The lawnmower that my dad hardly ever uses anymore. An old barbecue. A bunch of weed killer. My bike. I don't know why I'm back there, but there I am. I pull the bike out from all the junk. The chain has fallen off. It dangles uselessly. It takes me a while to fix it up. It's cold outside. I don't know why I'm doing it. I take it for a ride around the block. I'm wobbly at first. To tell you the truth, I get on and fall right off the other side and just lie there for a minute. But then I get going. I remember this, I think. I remember liking this.

I start riding to school. I know it's winter, but I don't care. Winter here is quirky. It's cold, sure, but the ice is melted by mid-morning and the sun hangs low in the sky in the afternoon and the air keeps a smattering of warmth. It doesn't snow, not much anyway, not enough to stop riding.

I used to ride all the time. I should say, we used to ride all the time. We did. We were kids, though. Kids don't drive, they don't take the bus, they ride their bikes. It's as simple as that. We would ride to Dan's to visit, we would ride to Trina's and to Ashley's. Sometimes all five of us would ride somewhere together, just for the sake of riding. For the sake of feeling strong, of being free. When you're a kid, you are far too much at the mercy of your parents or of whoever is giving you a ride to wherever you have to go. Bicycles were our ticket out.

Riding is my ticket out, now. Ticket out of what, I don't know.

I forgot how much I liked to ride to school, liked to arrive at school feeling refreshed and not feeling choked from the crowded bus. I know I go a bit crazy. I'm a bit compulsive, maybe. I start to ride a lot. I can't see it as a bad thing. I just can't. I ride to school. I ride before school and after school. It makes other things seem to matter less.

Sometimes, I get up really early and ride down to the beach and along the waterfront down to the very edge of the world. Sam and I used to go on that ride.

Of course we did.

Everything I do now is just a shadow of something I used to do with him, but now I'm doing it alone. I'm making it new. Everything feels new. It's me. I've been reborn. It's stupid, I know, but it makes me think about stuff. Spiritual stuff. Stuff about Sam and where he is now. And I feel so good on this pill, I want to do something for him. To remember.

Every day, I ride for Sam.

I get up at six in the morning. It's still dark — pitch dark — and when the alarm goes off it scares me. I lie in bed listening to my heart pounding, a familiar flapping in my chest. Only this time it's just the shock of adrenaline rushing through my veins, oxygen pumping through my lungs. When Sam first died, I stopped getting up early. I started sleeping until noon when I could get away with it. "Don't talk to her in the morning," my dad would say. "She's a grouch." In those days, it would be funny. He'd poke me with his spatula. "Grouch. Grouch." Now when he says it, it's cruel and hard.

Of course, if I wasn't already in a bad mood, I would certainly get there quickly with that sort of greeting. Or at least that's what I'd say. Sometimes he really made me mad. Not often, though. Usually I'd just fake it, to get a laugh. Mom would say, "Oh, leave her alone, Tony. Leave her alone if she's going to be a grouch."

The alarm goes at six. Every morning. I lie in bed until my eyes get used to the darkness, then I get changed. Dad bought me one of those flashing red lights to hook on to my sleeve so that cars can see me, so I attach that to my arm and step out the front door. When he gave it to me, he said it was so the angels could see me, could come and pick me up when I got run over by a car. "Whatever," I told him. "Don't be so goddamn optimistic."

"Don't swear," was all he said.

Well, screw him. I needed the light. Who am I to question his reasons? Maybe he just wants to believe in angels instead of ghosts. But I needed the light, he's right. Sometimes the cars swoop so close to you, that for a split second there is a possibility: a slight miscalculation and you could be lying in the road, a tiny error and the car could be over you.

The idea of that still doesn't scare me. The idea of being dead still hangs around in my thoughts, in the very farthest background of everything, like an echo.

It's almost the end of November now and it is pretty cold. Sharp. The kind of brittle cold that takes your breath away and stings your lungs. I have a Walkman, but I never listen to music when I ride. I like to be able to listen to the sounds of my own body. My breath rasping in and out, my heart pounding harder and faster. In a good way, not in the old, scary way. If I listen hard enough, I can almost hear my muscles getting stronger, my bones getting more prominent, my flesh flattening and smoothing out like marble.

Almost.

I have ridden for an hour every morning this week. Every morning I can go a bit farther, a bit faster. It's a race, you know? Against who, I haven't decided yet. I guess it's against me: old me and new me battling it out to see who gets to the end first.

It's Friday, a morning like any other and I'm riding towards the place where I know the sun will rise. There is nothing like the sight of that. It takes my breath away. But now it's still dark and cold and it's windy again and I'm listening for my body's sounds, my body's song, when I see a police cruiser driving down the road. There isn't any other traffic. This is a pretty quiet neighbourhood. At first I don't pay any attention, but then the number catches my eye: 888. Eight was Sam's lucky number. I don't even know why I noticed that little number on the police car, but I did. Eights. My heart does this extra lub-dup, and I think, what's that, why is it doing that. I think I might be having a panic attack, so I stop and rest on the curb for a minute. I close my eyes and open them again and look up into the dusky sky. The panic passes, if it was ever there. I lean over and adjust my pedal, so I have a reason to be stopped.

The car circles back and around and I get caught for a minute in its lights. It rolls to a stop right beside me. The house we are in front of has all the lights on inside. I should have noticed it before. It looks strange. One or two other houses have one or two lights on at this time of the morning, but no one's house is lit up like that, not unless they are having a party, and even then, it's too late or too early for that. These aren't party lights. They're death lights. I remember when Sam died, how the lights in our house were on all the time. How we couldn't sleep. How no one slept.

I keep standing there. I don't know why I do that. I can see movement through the living room window. The policeman gets out of the car, unfolds, really, because he is so tall. He looks over at me, but I don't think he really sees me. He looks past me into the dawn. The sky is just beginning to broaden a bit with colour. Probably, some-where behind me, the first sliver of the sun is visible. I stare at him. He is only a few feet from me, after all. I can hear him breathing. He is dark-haired with olive skin and a beard that might just be stubble on his chin. He looks Greek or Italian or something. I climb off my bike and fid-dle with my shoelaces on the sidewalk and he walks past me up to the house. It's so quiet that I can hear the door-bell reverberate, I can hear footsteps coming to the door. I stand up, so I can see it open, see a woman standing there in a robe, a man's robe, dark blue and flannel.

I can hear his voice. It's deep and solemn. I don't want to hear it. I can tell right away that I shouldn't be here. I shouldn't be witnessing something so private. So awful. He's saying something, what is he saying? He's saying, "I'm so sorry, Mrs. Wilson. I'm sorry. There's been an accident ..."

My heart starts beating like crazy, and all of a sudden Sam is back in my head again and I am on the edge of the mountain and he is letting go. I am waking up in the hospital and screaming, "Sam! Sam!"

"I'm sorry," the doctor is telling me, my dad is telling me, everyone is telling me. "I'm sorry ..."

This must be how Mom found out, I think. Someone must have come for her like this. Someone must have told her. It occurs to me that I don't know her story, I only know mine. I only know what it was like to cling there, to move my fingers and toes, to taste the end of the burned rope.

To be left alone.

I try to catch my breath and end up gasping like a person with asthma. I wobble a little, but I throw myself back onto my bike and start to ride. My blood has run cold, like little ice crystals are trying to pump through my heart.

I am riding. The night cracks open a bit, like an egg. The daylight is grey and murky.

I can't find the rhythm of pedalling. At the corner, I turn too fast and go over onto the pavement and my bike falls on top of me. It feels like slow motion, but my feet are stuck in the clips and I don't even try to stop myself from falling. I hit the ground hard. The white frost bites my cheek. I'm so startled that I start crying. My left knee hurts like crazy and my foot is half twisted out of its clip. My knee isn't broken, I can tell that much.

Not broken, but it hurts and I'm crying more from the shock than the pain. I'll have to walk home, I think. My bike is all bashed up and twisted. How could it be so mangled? What did I do? I must have pulled the frame as it was falling, I must have had super-human strength.

I'll be late. I don't want to panic, because a full-fledged panic attack will break the spell: the magic of the Prozac, the love of riding my bike. The fragile spell. Everything. I sit there on the freezing cold sidewalk and clutch onto my knee and try to will my body to get up, to get moving.

That's when the cop drives up. It's all unreal, like a stupid movie. I hate the feeling. I want to disappear. I'm caught in his headlights, and he pulls up beside me and gets out and is standing over me: "Are you all right? Do you need an ambulance?"

I keep my head down so he can't see my tears and I say, "It's just twisted, I'll be fine, I just need a minute."

"Where's your helmet?" he asks.

I shrug and try to stand up, but I can't. He reaches down and holds his hand out towards me, and I grab it and hoist myself up. We are standing facing each other at just the right angle to kiss. I know, it sounds ridiculous, but that's what I want to do. It's like there are magnets pulling us together. I gasp, but he doesn't seem to notice. We just stand there, staring, forever. I don't even think he's staring at my wonky eye. He seems to be looking right at me. Me. Like he is really seeing me. For a minute. One minute. He clears his throat and scratches his face.

He smells familiar. It must be cologne. He smells like someone I know, someone I've always known. What is it? I can't pinpoint it. He says, "At least let me give you a lift home."

So I do. He does. My bike is all crumpled up in the trunk of the car, car number 888. We don't say much in the car, but I find out his name. Joe. His name is Joe. He drops me off in front of my house, where there are lights on now upstairs because my parents are getting up for work, and I say, "Thanks."

"No problem," he says. Then he says, "Hey."

And I turn around, and he says, "Take care of you." That's exactly what Sam used to say. I swear he said it in Sam's voice. Not a kid's voice, but with his accent. His softness. And I think, this guy is a messenger, Sam sent him for me. I think, crazy Pagan. Don't go crazy. I close my eyes so I can't see birds or feathers. I close my mouth so nothing escapes.

He says, "Next time, don't forget your helmet."

I say, "Sure."

"I'm serious," he says. "I could fine you for not having one."

"Oh," I say.

"Besides," he says. "We wouldn't want you hitting that pretty face again."

Self-consciously, I reach up and touch my scratched cheek. It's tender under my touch, it will probably bruise and swell. Well, I've survived worse, I want to say, but he's already gone.

I float up to the door. I can't even feel my legs, much less my knee. I just drop my bike on the front lawn and leave it there.

When I get inside, of course, it's all a big catastrophe. "Hey, what happened to your leg?" Dad looks really worried, gets me some ice from the freezer. He looks like he thinks that I did it on purpose. I can't say I blame him, because of all the times I have hurt myself intentionally. What is he supposed to think?

"Oh, for God's sake," says Mom. "Really. How could you be so clumsy?"

Clumsy? I don't even know what to say to her. Now my knee is starting to hurt, and it has turned black and blue and is swelling up. I quickly take my little green pill. I know it isn't a pain pill, it just seems like a good idea.

"Nice, Mom," I mumble. "That's really fucking nice."

I don't mean to use that word. I mean, I use it all the time, but never to my mom. It's a big deal to her. I don't know why. It doesn't mean anything to me. There's this huge silence, and she goes out of the room, slamming the door. It isn't very effective because it's one of those swinging doors. Dad just sits there and watches it flap back and forth, like a giant wing.

"Shit happens," he says. "But you should watch your mouth."

"I guess," I say. I laugh. "Whatever." I hobble upstairs to get ready for school.

At lunch, I sit in the breezeway with Brett. She's smoking, and I'm eating some carrots that I've brought for lunch. She ate a donut and a Twinkie. "You're way too thin," she tells me, offering me some. But I still can't eat that kind of food. It just curdles in my stomach. I'm still not over that. I feel less crazy, but still sick. I tell her I can't.

"I can't eat sugar," I say. Which is true, right now, but not for any medical reason. I am getting thin. When I first started on the Prozac, when it first started to work, I wanted to eat everything, just for the taste. But then abruptly I lost interest. I don't care. I like my new shape. My body is tiny under my clothes, and I love the way it feels, light and hollow. I feel like I am made of that kind of gauze fabric that floats when you wear it. I feel like if you held me up to the light, you'd be able to see right through me. Like a ghost, a phantom.

We're sitting there, and this guy I haven't seen before comes up behind her and hugs her from behind.

"Hey," he says to me, as she jumps and yelps at him. "I still have your lighter. I think I might have lost it."

"Oh," I say. "Right. Doesn't matter." I don't really remember him, but it doesn't matter. Brett is grinning and I can tell that she likes him. Nathan. He's shorter than her, and stocky, with thick, blond hair that sticks up all over. He's such a boy.

Not like Joe.

She met him in shop class, that's what she's taking. She says, why not learn a trade if we're forced to waste our lives in school? I guess she's right. I should have taken shop instead of Algebra, or instead of Biology or History or Literature.

"Party tonight at my place," he says. He's smiling. He likes her. I can always tell these things. I can tell how people feel about each other. It's like they have a light around them that only I can see.

Brett says, "Great, we're in." We. What does that mean? Does that mean me? I still haven't been able to work up the nerve to invite myself along with her somewhere, in case I am just a "school" friend, just someone she was filling her time with while her real friends were somewhere else.

I should go, I think.

"I think I'm busy tonight," I say. She isn't listening. She's talking to someone else. I light another cigarette from the butt of my last one. My fingers are stained yellow. I haven't gone to a party since, well, since ever. Sam and I used to go to parties, sometimes, but we were thirteen. They were different types of parties. They were parties where someone's parents rented the skating rink and we all played hockey. They were parties where we played with Ouija boards and tried to scare each other by having séances and raising the dead. They weren't real parties. I guess I've been invited to them before, by other friends that I've had and then gradually lost over the last couple of years, friends I've treated badly enough that finally they stopped asking. I do kind of wonder what I've been missing. Now that I feel almost like a normal person, maybe I can have some fun. To tell you the truth, I'm kind of excited about the idea.

Nathan says "Cool" and reaches into his ripped jeans pocket to get out a little card that has his address printed on it.

"Very professional," says Brett, and laughs again. She's always laughing. For a second I hate her. Then I wonder if she's on Prozac, too. The idea scares me. All of us laughing together like crazy, the pills catapulting around in our blood, bubbling, making us all the same.

It's like a horror movie.

I get up and walk away. I drop my cigarette on the floor inside and it burns a hole in the waxed finish. I ignore it. I pretend I don't see it. That's the best way, I think. Just to pretend it didn't happen at all.

By the time the last bell goes, I'm starting to panic. People are talking about the party, people I only sort of know, from swimming and volleyball and from when we were kids. People who still look like strangers to me. I'm thinking that maybe I won't go. Why do I want to go? I go to my locker and grab a handful of books and stuff them into my knapsack. I think maybe I can duck out of here and avoid Brett. She'll understand, or likely she won't care. I'm hurrying out through the heavy doors and heading for the bus stop when Brett catches me and says, "You want to come to my place to get ready for the party tonight? Maybe you should stay over."

"Um," I say. "You know, I think I might have something I have to do tonight."

"Riddler," she says, winking at me. "Give me a break. See you at seven."

I think, okay, maybe that would work. Maybe I can do this.

I limp the rest of the way to the bus stop and then I hear a car honking like crazy and I look up and there is Dan in his too-big truck. "Want a ride?" he shouts over the sound of his stereo. I hesitate. I'm still mad at him.

"Hurry up," he says. "Get in."

I climb in. "You know, I read somewhere that people who listen to their stereo too loud end up in diapers because the bass tone affects their bowel muscles or something," I say. He doesn't even look at me, obviously because he can't hear me. The music is awful. How can he like this? I thought gay guys liked opera and classical, not gangster rap.

He reaches out and turns it off all of a sudden, and I swear I can hear it echo in my head.

"You look good these days," he says. "Where have you been? Are you mad at me?"

"I've lost some weight," I tell him. Hedging. "I've been riding my bike. I guess I've been busy."

"No," he says. "That isn't what I mean."

"I'm not so mad," I say.

"Good," he says. He doesn't ask me why. "You going to Nathan's tonight?"

"Yup," I say.

"You ARE?" he says, laughing. "You're kidding! You don't go to parties — everyone knows that."

"Everyone?" I say. I can't imagine that everyone cares what I do, to tell you the truth. The idea of them all sitting around and saying, "Oh, that Pagan never goes to parties," makes me feel strange.

"Don't be like that," he says. "I'm going too, maybe."

I guess everyone knew about it but me, which is no great surprise seeing as how I don't pay attention to very much. Dan is pretty antsy and he lights up a smoke.

"I shouldn't smoke in here," he says. "My dad will freak out."

"So don't smoke," I say. We are driving past the beach. He stops and gets out.

"Come for a walk," he says.

"My knee," I say, but then I think, why not? Who cares? We don't walk very far, just to the edge of the water. Instead of staring out into the sea, though, we turn and face the other way. It's cold and windy and the cigarette is the only thing that keeps me from freezing to death. My hand is shaking from the cold. From here, we can see across the street to this kindergarten at the church. There are kids all bundled up, playing in the playground. There is a teacher who is bending over one kid and tying his shoes. Then she straightens up and pushes them on the swings. We can hear them laughing and shrieking. For a second, I'm jealous. Not of the teachers, but of the kids. I remember what it was like to be that little, to not care about anything but swinging as high as possible on the swing set.

Suddenly, I feel about a thousand years old. We walk a little farther. It's muddy, and our feet sink into the ground. I have to be careful not to slip, I'm still limping pretty badly. Dan lights up another smoke and squints into the pale sun, and I swear he looks just like one of those old movie stars. Jimmy Dean or Humphrey Bogart. He's really very good-looking. It's too bad he's gay. He sits down in the wet, cold grass and says, "Tonight's the night."

"For what?" I say, thinking about the party. I sit down next to him. The ground is totally soggy, so I jump up and check out my pants to see if they are wet. He brushes the grass and mud off my leg.

"Tonight is what night?" I ask again.

"I'm going to tell him," he announces.

"Oh," I say. I don't know how to tell him that I really don't think it's a good idea. I mean, why make trouble? But I don't say anything, I just rest my hand on his shoulder. He's a football player, so he's got big shoulders. It's nice to be able to sit quietly without someone having to talk to fill the space. Dan and Brett are the only people that I have that with. It used to be Sam. We didn't have to talk. We had the same thoughts. I kind of pat Dan's arm, and we stay out there, smoking, not saying much. Smoking will kill us, probably, but who cares? Right?

That's how we both feel. It's how I feel anyway. I

don't feel so normal that I want to let go of my death fantasy. That's what Dr. K. calls it. A death "fantasy." He says I don't really want to die. He's probably right. On some level, I don't want to. But on another one, it seems like a good alternative.

CHAPTER 7

At home, I find Dad sitting at the kitchen table with a cup of cold coffee in front of him. I can tell it's cold because a bunch of the cream has sort of congealed on the top and it looks totally disgusting. I take it away and dump it down the sink, and he says, "Thanks, Pagan."

I don't ask him why he wasn't at work, though it's pretty obvious he didn't go. Sometimes, he has days like this. I understand. I know exactly how he feels. The house is quiet, so Mom is still at her job. She works at the phone company. Actually, I have no idea what she does there. Something important, no doubt. Something where she gets to dress up and boss people around. Dad is in real estate. He doesn't sell it, he just sort of buys a lot of it and then makes money building stuff, like hotels and apartments. He is usually working all the time. He says that he is a workaholic. He just loves to work. He gets these days every once in a while, days when he can't stop thinking about what happened. I can relate to that. Still, I don't want to know what he is feeling. I know he's thinking about Sam. And, obviously Bob. Bob died, too, and he was Dad's brother. They weren't twins, not like me and Sam. Not like us.

There is this big silence. I don't know what to do with it. I sit down across from him and trace my scars. Tap my patch. He looks at me. He doesn't look angry today, just deflated. We both talk at once, I'm asking him: "Can I go out tonight?"

And he is saying, "How's your knee?"

I say, "It's okay, it's a little swollen, but I was wondering could I stay at Brett's tonight?"

And he laughs this sharp little laugh like a knife blade, and says, "Who's Brett, your new boyfriend?"

I say, "No, Dad, she's a *girl*."

"Oh," he sighs. Sometimes when he sighs it's like all the air has just poured out of him and he sits there, empty. " Okay," he says. "You can go."

It was easier than I thought, which is good. But at the same time it makes me feel uncomfortable that I didn't exactly tell him the whole truth, about the party. I know Mom probably wouldn't have let me go. She likes to meet all my friends and grill them about their lives before I am so much as allowed to see a movie with them. Or at least she used to do that. I haven't really had any friends for a long time.

Not that she's noticed.

Not that she's seen how alone I've been.

I know she'll be mad that I left before she got home from work, but I don't care. I don't. She can take it up with her stupid group and they can hug her and tell her how awful I am and then they will all feel better.

I walk over to Brett's house because I don't want to ask Dad for a ride. My knee hurts like hell but I don't care. The pain is familiar, comforting. There isn't anything I can do about it. It's out of my control. Brett lives on the other side of the school. I really should have taken the bus, at least half way. I haven't taken a bus for ages. I've been riding my bike instead. The bus goes by, all lit up like a fish tank. The people are looking out the windows but seeing nothing. I'm glad not to be on it, breathing their tired exhalations. My knee throbs but I like how cold the air is on my face. It's really dry, and I can tell that my hair is going to get static. That always happens when it gets cold. Sometimes I rub dryer sheets on it, to keep the static down. Sam's hair was like mine. It got really wild in the winter. It was so straight and fine, it would just stick out all over the place. Before he died, he was getting more self-conscious about it. He was just barely fourteen. But he was starting to notice stuff — like what his hair looked like. I teased him about it, but I wish I hadn't. It made him blush. He had started gluing it down with hair gel. Mom called him "Helmet Head," because he used so much goo that it hardened almost into plastic. He hadn't used any on the day he fell, though. I remember how his hair was blowing in the wind. I remember how the sun shone on it.

I can feel the air crackling by my ears. They hurt a little when the wind blows into them. I wish I'd thought to bring a scarf, but I guess that would have looked pretty stupid. The leaves that are on the ground are crisp and dead. With each footstep I take, there is a crunching sound, like bones breaking. It's dark. I feel kind of uneasy, but not scared. Not really. The dark doesn't bother me too much. Not more than anything else, anyway. The only sound is my feet, crunching the brittle dead leaves, and that's all.

Snow crunches like that, I think to myself. I think about walking in the snow, and there it is again. The avalanche. I start to get sad. Scared. The grief wells up and I swallow it down. Swallow again. I stop walking and try to pull myself together. The problem with walking is that I think too much. Think of something else, I tell myself. Think of Joe. I try to imagine him walking beside me. I imagine telling him stories about Sam. I try to think of one from when we were all together, me and Sam and Mom and Dad, but I can't. It's like there is a big hole there, in all my good memories, where Sam must have been. I feel a little panicky. Why can't I remember? Is it this stupid pill? Is it making me forget?

I try to slow down and concentrate. I remember this one time when Sam and I went out for Halloween dressed up as Elvis impersonators. We were about seven. Mom was a big fan. We wore these white sequined outfits stuffed with pillows. We must have looked hilarious. Mom drew sideburns on our cheeks with eyeliner. Sam kept singing little bits of Elvis songs in exchange for the candy. He had a really good voice. He could really sing. When we got home, he gave me all his candy because he never liked chocolate. When he got older, he said he was allergic, but I think he was actually just the only person in the world who didn't like it.

I feel better now. I'm walking along and my feet are kicking through the dead leaves, and I suddenly think to myself that maybe it would be easier to be crazy, to just let it all slip away. It would be like getting on a boat and floating downstream. Just floating, letting the current take me wherever. Anywhere but here.

By the time I get to Brett's, I'm shivering. It's getting really cold. Her mom and dad are out, and the nanny is there looking after her little sister, Daisy. She was named after a character in a Fitzgerald novel. Their dad is some big writer or something. I've never heard of him, but Brett says he's famous. That's cool, I guess. I wish my dad were famous, or my mom. Something to make them less obvious, less ordinary. I take one look at her sister and know right away that even though she is cute, there is something wrong with her. Her eyes are a little too close together, and her head is a little too big. Also, her mouth hangs open a little bit. She's a pretty girl though, like a tiny version of Brett, and she comes right over and hugs my legs. Kids are great. They don't let the eye patch faze them at all. Adults are usually more weird about it.

The nanny sort of pulls her off me and laughs. She speaks to Daisy in another language. Filipino, I think. I guess Brett's mom must be Filipino, too. Maybe that explains why Brett is so dark and exotic-looking. She tells me right away, when the nanny takes Daisy away. She says, "She's retarded, but we have to pretend not to notice because Mom doesn't believe it's true." She makes a loopy gesture with her finger.

"That's kind of strange," I say.

She just laughs. "Whatever gets you through the day," she says. "Whatever makes it easier."

And, I think, maybe she's right. Maybe that's what Dad is doing, just trying to get through the day. That's what Mom is doing, by working all the time and snapping at me and bitching at Dad. Maybe that's what I am doing, by seeing Dr. Killjoy and taking pills.

I feel a bit weird being here. It's been a long time since I've been in someone else's house. This is a nice house, though, and she is so relaxed that it's hard for me to stay nervous. I end up borrowing a pair of her jeans and a black top that is really short, so you can see my whole stomach. I'm surprised these things fit. I guess I thought of Brett as this little small person, whereas I thought of myself as more of a great big oaf. But I guess I know that I'm shrinking. For some reason, I think of that shirt I stole earlier this year. I still have it. I keep it in my drawer with all my other shirts, but I've never worn it. I guess I could get away with wearing it now, if only it were summer outside. Now that I'm small. Now that I'm half of what I used to be. I don't mean that about my weight, I mean that I'm only half a person without Sam, and now I am even less than that. I don't want to think about that now, but I can't stop. Why isn't this stupid pill working? My hands are starting to sweat, so when Brett offers me a beer, I take it and take a long drink from the bottle. I think about nothing but the wheat and yeast taste of the beer and how the bubbles burn a little and about how beer smells so different from how it tastes. Brett helps me do my hair, and I just sit there and let her brush it and blow dry it and somehow when she is finished, it isn't all plastered down on my scalp. Instead it looks thick and clean and healthy and I think, hey, I actually look pretty good. Not like myself, like a stranger. A good-looking stranger. With an eye patch.

Brett's wearing a red dress that is a bit too tight, but it's dark crimson red, not cheap and bright, and it's made of the same material as T-shirts, so it's not too dressy. Over that, she's wearing a black leather jacket that she got at a used clothing store, or that's what she says. She actually said, "It's just thrift junk, don't look at it like that." I sort of don't believe her. I can tell from this house that she has money, but that maybe it embarrasses her. Maybe that's why she didn't invite me here before.

She looks really cool. I look at us standing side by side in the mirror and we look really similar, except my hair is long and blonde and hers is long and black and curly. And she has blue eyes, and mine are green. Well, one of them is, anyway, the only one that shows.

"Lookin' good, girlfriend," she says, grabbing my hand. "Let's go party!"

And I think, this isn't really me. But I let myself get dragged along in the current anyway. I mean, it might not be *me*, but it feels okay. It must be all right. We're all just trying to fit in, aren't we? Just trying to blend in with the crowd.

We walk to the party, which isn't that far away, and Brett keeps talking about how cold it is, and how she can hardly stand it. She's smoking her brains out to try to keep her lungs warm, but I draw the cold air into my lungs and think that maybe I like the cold because my heart is ice. All this cold air is comforting to it, or at least familiar to my frozen heart. The moon is out. It's huge in the sky, and the trees are silhouetted against it. It's so quiet and still except for the odd car roaring by on the wet road, and I think, this is beautiful. This is perfect. It's nice to walk, and to be quiet.

It's nice not to be afraid, or sad.

It's nice not to have to fake it.

With Trina and Ashley, there was always chatter. "He said this, and I said this, and she said this, and I go, and he goes, and she goes." It didn't even mean anything half the time, it was just noise to fill the gaps. I guess we were all pretty young, then, thirteen. I guess maybe they have changed, too. I've kind of ignored them this year. And last year. And the year before that. I know I'm being a bitch, but I just can't help it. I need to be by myself. I don't want people fawning over me all the time. With Brett, I don't have that. She smokes and I smoke and think about stuff, and we're okay, just like that.

She doesn't know about Sam. That's the best part. She doesn't care.

The party is in this weird little basement suite in this big old house that looks haunted. Well, maybe not haunted, but it sure looks like it hasn't been painted in about a hundred years, and the grass is all overgrown with weeds and vines. It's probably what our house looked like before Mom and Dad fixed it up. There are a lot of houses like that here. This is an old city. Everything is old: the trees, the houses, the families, the stories. Same old, same old.

We go around the back, and I start to feel nervous and my stomach sort of flip-flops like it does when I get uptight. Like it's been doing on and off all day. Brett is perfectly relaxed. She doesn't knock, just goes right in like she owns the place and I follow, because why not. I can do that, too. There's a few people standing around in the kitchen, which is the first room we come into. They're drinking and laughing and all of a sudden I feel this wave of relief, because for the first time in a long time, everyone is having a good time and no one is looking over at me and saying, gee, there's that girl with the dead brother. If they're looking, it's because of the patch. It does set me apart.

It's refreshing, really. That's what I would call it. I don't know any of these people, and they all look as though they are probably older than us, but that's okay, too. I wonder where everyone from school is, I wonder where Dan is. I don't mind too much. Sometimes it's easier to disappear in a room full of strangers than in one that's full of acquaintances or people you used to know.

Brett walks over to the fridge and takes out two beers and brings one to me. We go deeper into the apartment. It looks like there are maybe a hundred people crammed into the living room. I can see that Brett is wanting to spend some time with Nathan, alone, so I move away from them a little and let myself get dragged into the smoky, noisy crowd. It's a bit like diving into a pool, once you're in the water, it's a lot easier than you thought it would be. And a lot warmer. I drink my beer and let the room get lighter and more meaningless, and I flip my hair around, and you know what else?

I start talking to people. And laughing.

I talk to some really cute guys. I even give my number to one of them, whose name is Chance. I write it on a matchbook, and I say, "Are you going to take a chance on calling this number?", which is something way more flirtatious than what I would usually say.

And he laughs and whispers, "Do you feel like taking a Chance?"

It's corny, but I think, okay. What the hell. I step back and look at him. He's a little taller than me, and has brown hair that sort of flops over one eye, and his eyes are small and grey, like steel. Cold. I like that. He doesn't look like someone who would be nice and kind and sentimental. He doesn't look like someone who would want to know my life story. I let him talk to me some more. I let myself get pulled closer to him by the crowd and the beer. And when he says, "Here, try this," I do. I mean, I'm not that kind of person. I used to be scared of drugs of any kind, but he says, "Don't worry, it's herbal."

So I do it. Why not? I swallow pills every day. And suddenly the colours are brighter, and we're dancing and dancing and I feel like I do when I'm riding my bike, like I can't stop, because if I do stop then I'll stop breathing. And I'm dizzy and calm at the same time. I feel like I'm not really there, but I am. The same old feeling as I get sometimes, but different, more explosive. I can't explain it. I'm not describing it right.

We dance until the sun comes up. We go outside and dance in the snow in the yard. I think we might even kiss. I think I remember his lips, soft and wet and warm, like a memory you can't quite bring into focus all the way. I think I remember that he ran his finger along my naked stomach and goose bumps came up in the path of his touch. I might remember him doing that. I might remember letting him.

Sometimes when we're dancing I think I hear this little voice in my head, like Sam's voice, saying: "You're not ready for this; this isn't you. You aren't ready for this. You aren't ready." But it's easy not to listen, with all the music and the people and the drugs. I'm really busy trying to forget, so I don't listen. I can't.

I mean, I'm dancing.

I haven't danced in a long time.

My ears hum and echo all the next day, long after we go back to Brett's and crash out on her bed. Long after I leave her house and walk home, feeling kind of sick and kind of happy at the same time. Long after my Dad passes me a note saying that Chance called, and wants me to call back.

He doesn't even ask who Chance is.

There's still an echo in my head when I go to bed. It's only five o'clock in the afternoon, but I can't stay awake. I can hear my heart thudding over the sound of the buzz in my ears, and for a minute I get scared — I think, what did I do? I can hear Mom yelling at me from far away, calling me to come and clean up the music room or help with dinner, or something. But I can't stay awake, I can't think about it right now. I am so tired that I don't think that I dream anything at all.

I am falling asleep when I think: Dan. I didn't see him last night at all. Was it that he was going to tell his Dad? I don't remember. I remember a conversation. I don't remember what he said. I should call him. I pick up the phone. The screen glows green in the half-light. I try to think of his number, but I can't. Numbers fill my head, numbers that aren't phone numbers: 113, the amount I weigh; 01/14, the day Sam died; 888, Joe's car number. I can't think straight. Dr. Killian's answering machine pops into my head: 250-555-6789.

Dan, I think. Where are you? But it's too late, you see. I'm falling asleep. I can't fight that. I'm so tired. The dreams start before I even close my eyes. The phone becoming something else and becoming something else and becoming …

And then I'm gone. It's too late.

I'm a bad friend.

In the morning, when I wake up, I've forgotten about it. I'm thinking instead about Chance. A boy who likes me. I'm smiling into my cereal. I'm thinking that it's going to be okay.

Stupid me. Crazy me. What do I know about anything, really?

CHAPTER 8

The halls at school gleam and smell of floor wax. I'm early. Slip through the metal detectors, unnoticed. Not that I have any metal. The detectors were put in last year when someone brought a lighter to school that was shaped like a gun. He stood in the breezeway with it and lit cigarettes. Some kids freaked out. It was too soon after what happened at Columbine. People were still expecting to come to school and be shot in a spray of bullets. I never thought it could happen here. I still don't.

The metal detector stays silent as I pass through the doorway it makes in the hall. There are a few other kids around. Kids I don't know. I go to my locker. I can't think of the combination. What's wrong with me? All the numbers are going. Maybe this is how I start to forget. Maybe it starts with numbers. I take a deep breath and spin the lock. Spin it and spin it and stop. It opens.

I'm okay, I think to myself. *I'm fine.*

Last night on the phone, Chance said, "Will you meet me after school? Will you come over?"

"Sure," I said. "I'd love to."

I'm nervous. In my locker, I have a tiny mirror. In it,

I see a blemish on the cheek of my reflection. A zit. I comb my hair forward and strands of it fall to the floor. Dr. Killian is right. I am too self-involved. I sit down on the floor and pull a book out of my locker and stare at the pages. I have a history test today … or a biology test. I don't remember which.

Chance, I think. *Like me, like me, please like me.*

I look up, and Dan is coming down the hall. I recognize him as he passes through the metal detector. I recognize the shape of his walk.

Dan, I think. Where were you? I'm getting ready to ask. I'm on my feet, looking. He walks by me, without turning his head. His face bruised and black circles around his eyes. His nose obviously broken.

"Morning," he says, not stopping.

"Morning," I say, following him, my locker hanging open in the hall. I don't care. Let them steal my purse. There's nothing in it. Emergency tampons that I never need. A change purse full of coins. My cigarettes are in my pocket. That's all that matters.

"What …?"

"Don't," he says. "Not now."

"God, Dan," I say, "you have to tell me. Tell me now. Dan. Come on."

"I don't want to talk about it," he says. His hand is trembling. I want to reach out and hold it, but I don't because he's gay. As though gay people don't want to be comforted. Stupid, I think. I touch his arm.

"Did you tell your Dad?" I say.

"Duh," he says. "No kidding. Look, do you want to get out of here?"

History test, I think. College grades, I think. My

mouth is moving.

"Absolutely," I say. I don't even go back to my locker. Maybe someone will close it for me. I don't care.

Dan doesn't have the truck. The place where it is usually parked is empty. He starts to walk down the street, fast, and I walk next to him. It's cold. I have to take small, running steps to keep up.

"I wish you were Sam," he says suddenly. His breath hangs in front of him, so I can see what he said for longer. I'm so surprised I don't say anything.

"Fuck," he says. "I didn't mean that."

"Sam was a good listener," I say. "When he wasn't up to something."

"Yeah," he says. "I guess that's what I meant to say." We walk without saying anything. Up streets and down. I don't know what time it is. I left my watch in my locker. Well, that's probably gone now too. I light a cigarette and offer him one but he shakes his head. Mine rests between my fingers and keeps me company.

"He said I was sick," he says finally. "He said he'd pay to get me cured. Hey, maybe I should see your shrink. Not that he's helping you."

"Dr. Killian," I say carefully. My voice is tiny cubes of ice. "I think he's helping me."

"I didn't mean that," he says. "I'm just being an asshole. I don't know what's wrong with me."

I don't either, I think. I'm shivering. I need a new winter coat, but I haven't asked Mom for the money. She doesn't seem to notice yet that my two-year-old coat is too small. The sleeves come down to a spot three inches above my wrists. I rub my scars. Because I'm cold. Because it's a habit.

"Let me start again," he says. "I'm sorry, Pagan."

I shrug. "Forget it," I say. "I'm sure I've said worse things."

"Not to me," he says. "You've never been anything but a friend to me."

I didn't call you, I think. *What kind of friend doesn't call?*

"He hit me," Dan says. That part is obvious. "He hit me with the phone. One of those ugly old black phones. It weighs about five pounds. I can't believe he hit me with that. I can't believe he hit me. He's my father. My own father. I can't believe it. I can't believe he did that."

"The phone," I say.

"It fucking rang while he was pummeling me with it," he says. "I wonder who was on the other end." He smiles a bit. A dry smile with no warmth in it. "I wonder what it sounded like to him."

We walk a while further. On our left, there is a vacant lot that is filled with blackberry bramble and trash. On either side of it, there are beautiful houses with manicured lawns. Perfect lines where they stop cutting and the ugliness begins. I think, if that was my house, I'd fix that lot up just so I didn't have to look at it. A wasp who should be dead by this time of year slowly wobbles by towards the thicket.

"What are you going to do?" I ask. We stop walking and sit down on the sidewalk, our feet resting on the street. This is a quiet street. We sit for a long time and no cars go by. No bikes. No people. The sky is grey-blue and streaked with long white strands of stretched cloud. I try to stop my legs from shivering. I try not to look eager to move.

"I'm going to leave," he says. "I mean, I already left. My mom told me to. She said that he couldn't deal with it. That I would have to go. That I had to get out. Because of him. Why didn't he have to leave?"

"Fuck," I say. It's the only thing I can think of. "Where are you going to go?"

"I'm staying with my cousin," he says. "Garry. I don't even know the guy. I have to sleep in his goddamn room on a mattress on the floor. My aunt just has this really tiny place. She sleeps in the living room and I sleep on Garry's floor. Like we're six years old and having a sleepover."

"I know Garry," I say. "Doesn't he go to our school?"

"Yeah," Dan says. "He's the computer guy. Guy most likely to come to school and shoot us all for picking on him when we were ten. I'm sleeping on his floor." He pulls his shirt and looks at it. I didn't notice it before. It's one of those rock shirts with a band's name and flames. "I'm wearing his stupid, ugly shirt."

"Oh," I say. "Man." I light another cigarette, just for the warmth. The sun is right overhead, but it's too weak to be warm.

I feel so sad. "Let's not go back," I say. "Let's go to the mall. I need a new coat."

"You're freezing," he says. Finally looking at me. "You're shivering."

"I'm always cold," I say. "Don't worry about it."

The mall is just around the corner. We've come a long way. Inside, it is sterile and warm. I start sweating right away. We must look like quite a pair. I am still limping a bit and wearing my eye patch, and his face looks like a war zone, as my dad would say. I wouldn't say it. I'm a child of the nineties. We have no war to relate to.

Dan picks up a shoe from a display. Weighs it in his hand.

"Can I help you?" a guy says. He's wearing a black-and-white striped shirt. He looks embarrassed to be there.

"No," says Dan. "I doubt it."

The day slips by. We have coffee in the coffee shop that faces the parking lot, sitting at a table on the sidewalk. It is cold and looks stormy, so we are the only people out here. I push my chair close to the table because it seems it will be warmer that way, and I wrap my hands around my coffee cup.

"I met someone," I tell him. "At that party."

"Who?" he says. But he isn't really listening when I try to tell him. He's staring off across the street. His eyes are red. I can't tell if he's crying or if it's just from the black eyes. He kind of nods and smiles, but he isn't smiling all the way, just smiling to show interest that he obviously doesn't feel.

"Forget it," I tell him. "I don't want to talk about it." I light a cigarette and pull it so deeply into my lungs that I start to choke, muffling it into my sleeve. I don't know why I smoke, I really don't. I don't even like it.

We just sit there and stare at people walking by. In the middle of the day there are lots of old people inside having coffee. They make me feel sad. They always look so alone. Their faces just light up when they see someone that they know or when someone stops and says hello.

"How's Brett?" Dan says, out of the blue. He's twisting the paper sleeve that came around his cup.

"Good," I say. He doesn't like her, I know he doesn't. I can just tell.

"Huh," he says. "I'll bet she is."

"What's that supposed to mean?" I say.

"Nothing," he says.

"You don't like her," I say. "Don't worry, I get it."

"I don't not like her," he says. "I just don't, well, I don't know. Forget it."

For a second, I can imagine having this conversation with Sam. If he didn't like my new friend, he'd probably act just like this. Or would he? I don't even know. It wasn't an issue, before. We just had friends and didn't worry about who liked who. Everyone just liked everyone else.

"Why don't you like her?" I ask. "I think she's cool."

"She's an idiot," he says. "She's a slut."

"What do you know?" I say. "You're gay."

He just stares at me for a minute, like I've hit him. "That doesn't mean I can't tell what she's like. I've heard stuff. Just because I'm gay doesn't mean, well, Jesus. Forget it. You like her, that's great. Be happy."

I get up and go back inside for a refill. I've been drinking so much coffee lately. It can't be good for me, but I don't much care. I wait while the girl makes it, steaming the milk and so on. I try to imagine myself doing that. She doesn't look much older than me. Maybe this is the kind of job I'll have to get if I don't go to college. She doesn't look unhappy. My parents would look down on her, but who cares? She has a job, she gets to listen to good music and make people happy all day. She gets to talk to these old people and make them smile and she gets to forget all about it when she leaves.

I take a big sip of my drink at the counter, to stop it

from overflowing, and I burn my lips and tongue. I hate that feeling. Through the window, I can see Dan flinging his empty cup up and down. I wish my friends could like each other, you know? But I guess everything can't always go the way you want it to go.

I go back outside, and I don't say anything. I sip my coffee and he smokes and we flick little crumbs to these tiny birds that are hopping around on the sidewalk. Then something happens. I look up and I see Joe.

I look up and see him standing there, and I swear my heart just stands still. I guess I gasp, and he looks down and smiles and says, "Pagan, right? How's that knee?"

"Good," I mumble, like an idiot. "Fine, it's great. How are you?"

"Pretty good," he says. He looks right into my eye and I can feel it all the way down to my knees. Then, he just kind of gives a little wave salute and walks into the coffee shop. I stare at him as he leans on the counter, talking to the girl there. I feel jealous. Just for a second, until he takes his coffee, comes back out through the door and winks at me. Then I feel like the only person in the world.

"Who was that?" Dan asks, staring at Joe as he gets into his cop car, number 888.

"Just a friend," I say, but I can tell I am blushing. The heat creeps up my cheeks in a wave.

"Not bad," Dan says. "Not bad at all." For a second, I can't figure out what he is talking about, and then I realize he is talking about Joe. Dan thinks Joe is good-looking. I laugh a little.

"What's funny?" he demands.

"Nothing," I tell him. But I want to say, you're funny.

I mean, being gay isn't funny or anything, it just seems weird that a *guy* would be attracted to the same person that I am. I know he's gay. I get it. It's just that I can't quite get my head around the whole idea of it. I wonder if Sam would have still been his friend once he knew. I can't say he would have been. I don't know. He used to make fun of Boy George, I remember that. He used to laugh at him.

I look over at Dan and touch his hand and think, why is it all so difficult? Why can't anything just be easy?

We don't say much. Wander in and out of stores like we have forever to just look at things. There is one shop that has a piano in it. The store sells china, crystal, that kind of crap. I don't know why they have a piano, but I sit down at it. I start to play. I play Dan a song that I know he likes. I forget what it's called. It's from a movie. Theme song. I play and I play. He stands there, listening, and then when I'm halfway through "The Moonlight Sonata," he walks out and leaves me there alone. I don't go after him. I finish the piece and then I leave. I go calmly into the department store and find the coat department. I take a pile of coats to a mirror in the corner and try them on. They are all the same. Long, wool coats. I put one on then another then another. I keep putting them on and taking them off. No one offers to help. It's so easy to put on one that wasn't mine to begin with, twist off the shoplifters tag, ripping the smallest of holes along the seam of the sleeve. So easy to walk out the door, heart racing, walk out onto the street and see that it's dark.

It's dark.

Chance, I think. And I start to run.

Too late, too late, too late. I don't know where he

lives. He was going to pick me up after school. I run all the way to the school, my new coat soaking in my sweat, but the parking lot is empty. I've screwed up.

I call him. "I'm sorry," I say.

"I forgive you," he says. He's drunk, I can tell. His words slur. "Come over now." He gives me his address.

"I can't," I tell him. But he's already hung up.

An hour later, he calls back.

"I'll pick you up after school tomorrow," he says. "Don't be late again."

"Okay," I say. I hate myself for feeling grateful. I hate him. I like him. I want him to like me. I pick out some clothes to wear. The right clothes, something perfect.

I tell Mom. "I have a date tomorrow after school." I say it casually.

"A date?" she says.

"Yes," I say.

"Oh, Pagan," she says. "All grown up. Don't be late for dinner."

"Okay," I say. I don't know why I was expecting more.

I'm late for swimming in the morning, late for school, late for biology, but when the teacher asks me why, I just shrug. I find it's better not to talk. They don't press you for answers if you look away. On the lab benches, there are trays of tiny emerald frogs. We're expected to cut them open. The scalpel tugs their skin and doesn't open them. I have to wait for the teacher to do mine for me, I can't break through. Inside, instead of being red with blood, the frog's organs are grey and withered. I label its heart with a pin and a paper tag. It's simple, really. The insides of us, our heart and brain and whatever, that's simple. It's all the other things, the feelings — that part is the hard part. I remind myself to tell Dan that, but it sounds cheesy, even when I think it, so I know I won't.

After school, I look all over the place for Brett. To tell her about Chance. She isn't there. I go and wait in the parking lot for him but he isn't there either. I go back inside. It's hard to find anyone in this big mass of people. The halls after school are crazy, mayhem. All the shouting and lockers banging and books being tossed into bags and cell phones ringing. Pagers beeping. Sometimes I just feel like going into the washroom and hiding there until the crowds have gone. Until it's safe. But today, I throw myself into the current and look for Brett. She's the only one I can talk to about Chance, and I'm bursting to talk to someone. I can't find her and no one has seen her. I think that's pretty strange. I didn't see her all day. I think about going over to her house, but I've only been there once and that might be too weird.

A car honks its horn. For me? I think. For me.

And there he is. He is such a boy. I can't remember what happens next. We go to his house, I guess. We sit and listen to music. He touches my hand. He kisses me. It gets dark.

He kisses me.

Finally, I have to go. My heart is singing. *He likes me, he likes me, he likes me*. I feel euphoric. I have no one to tell.

Brett, I think.

Dr. Killjoy, I think, and that's when I remember I was

supposed to see him today. It's the first appointment I've ever missed.

It's cold and the wind is blowing hard. The fallen leaves whip against the sides of buildings, pile up in grates. The trees snap and creak. Whole branches blow across the street. I pass a fire truck pulling a branch off a wire, sparks showering down onto the pavement. I go the long way home, walking.

When I get home, I hear voices upstairs. Not loud voices, but I notice them, mostly because there is a strange car in the driveway. The voices seem out of place. Too loud. Too present. I get the idea that I don't want to know what they are saying. I grab an apple from the bowl and crunch down on it. The white flesh is veined with pink. I concentrate on that. Tune the voices out. I put the water on to boil for spaghetti.

I hear the sound of high heels on the stairs. I guess I assume it is Mom. I mean, who else would it be? I go into the hallway. It isn't Mom. It takes me ages to figure it out. I'm standing in her way. She can't get past me. The hall is narrow and long. I lean against the wall.

"Oh, hi," I say, swallowing bile. Swallowing feathers. "What are you doing here? Aren't you my dad's secretary?" I challenge her with my eye. My hand is shaking, I can see it but I can't stop it. I touch my patch with my shaking hand that doesn't seem like mine. I stroke it. She's looking. I can tell she's uncomfortable. Good. She should be. *Get out*, I think. *Get out, get out, get out.* "Is my dad okay?" I ask, faking innocence, pretending to not know why she is here, why her cheeks are so pink. I know that he is okay. I know that it's obvious what she's doing here but I'm not going to let her off that easily. My heart is beating high in my throat. Making me talk.

"What are you doing here?" I repeat. I feel like I could repeat it forever. Until she answers.

"Hi Pagan," she says. Her face is a mask. Blank. She fits right in around here, I think. We're big on masks.

"What are you doing here?" I say. I don't move. I want her to understand. I have forever to stand here and ask. And ask and ask and ask. She looks around at the space above my head. Her mask cracks slightly and a flush creeps up her cheeks.

"How are you?" she tries. "Your dad has been so worried about you, what with …" .

"What are you *doing* here?" I say. The hands on the clock jump forward a notch. She twitches. She twitches and I shake. It's funny if you think about it, the two of us standing here, vibrating. I suddenly understand the expression "cut the tension with a knife."

"Oh," she says. "I was just … leaving."

"Uh huh," I say. Her face collapses. Her lip trembles. It's enough. I feel like I'm going to be sick. I'm dizzy. I push by her and get a whiff of really flowery perfume. I'm choking on it. I wish I'd pushed her harder. I go into the music room, the first room I see. Dust everywhere, the piano silent. I sit on the bench and touch the keys. I try to play as loudly as possible. I play all the loud crashing pieces I can think of and then I play the guitar in wild riffs. Inside me, something snaps. I hear a howl-ing. I think it's me. Are my lips moving? I feel like an animal. I don't know where the howl is coming from, but it's like I can't stop. It sounds like screaming. I can tell Dad is watching me through the little glass window in the door, but I don't care. Why should I?

What is he doing to us?

Fuck you, I say to his silhouette in the glass. *Fuck you and fuck you and fuck you.*

I guess he doesn't care. I thought it was coming back together. I thought he was going to that goddamned group.

I guess he doesn't care about this stupid, half-assed family of ours.

He stands there for a long time. I ignore him. I am finally finished, deflated like a flat tire, spent. And he is gone.

When Mom gets home, we sit down and eat and make small talk. The noodles are overcooked and stick to my teeth. She doesn't eat hers, she stirs it around. "How was your date?" she asks.

"It wasn't really a date," I say. "We just hung out and talked."

"Oh," she says. "I remember dates like that."

She doesn't ask me about him. We both carefully avoid mentioning Dad. It's easy, actually. She's made it easy, this kind of lying. We have been not mentioning Sam for years, pretending he didn't exist. This is old hat. Everything feels both really strange and really normal. I try to tell her about Biology, about the frog and how simple it was inside, but it comes out wrong. It's ruined by talking about it. "That's disgusting," she says. "Let's not talk about that while we are eating."

It's all such bullshit anyway. I don't know what I'm saying. I switch to talking about the weather. I feel myself starting to get more and more anxious. I'm babbling. My voice goes on and on. I can barely hear it myself. There is so much tension in the room, it makes it hard to breathe. My heart is beating faster and faster and I'm galloping through space and I'm trying to remember if I took my little green pill today. I take another one just in case.

"What's that?" Mom says.

I shake my head. "Nothing," I say. "Prozac."

"Oh," she says. She looks sad. She looks down at her plate.

I push my chair back from the table. It squeals on the tile. She looks up.

"My knee feels so much better," I tell her. "I'm just going to go for a quick ride."

"But it's dark," Mom says. "You'll hurt yourself."

"Honestly, Mom," I say. "Give me a break for once, would you?"

"Give *you* a break," she repeats. "Give you a break. When is someone in this family going to give *me* a fucking break?" She's crying a bit, tears sliding down her cheeks. Sorry. I can't deal with it. Sorry, sorry, sorry. I don't stick around to hear the rest. I grab my bike and roll off down the street, pedalling faster and faster until I can't really tell how much my knee hurts anymore.

I ride all the way over to Brett's and ring the doorbell. Her mom answers. I've never seen her before. She is tiny and has this wild hair that is all arranged perfectly on her head in this elaborate swirl. She goes to the hairdresser a lot, I remember Brett told me. She doesn't work because her husband is so famous and rich. Whatever.

"I love your hair," I tell her. "I'm Pagan. Is Brett home?"

"Who are you?" she asks.

"I'm Brett's friend, Pagan," I say again.

"Who's Brett?" she says.

"Um, your daughter?" I try.

"Brett?" she laughs. "Is that what she calls herself? Brett?" She laughs just the same way that Brett does. "That's funny," she says finally. "Brett. Let me get her for you."

Brett comes down and pushes her mom out of the way and comes out to the porch with me. She looks like she is in a really bad mood and I am almost sorry I came.

"What's the matter?" I ask.

"Did she tell you?" she says, poisonously.

"Tell me what?"

"My name," she hisses.

"Um, no," I tell her. And then I say, "Besides, what difference if she did?"

"I hate my name," Brett says moodily and kicks the balcony with her bare foot. She glares at me. I feel uncomfortable. It occurs to me that I don't know her at all, not really. I don't even know her name, or why she changed it, or anything at all.

"You must be freezing," I say. "I just came by to see why you weren't in school today."

"Oh," she shrugs. "That was nice of you. Weird, but nice. I guess the nanny is sick or whatever and I had to stay home with Daisy."

"Oh," I say. I think of all the things I want to tell her, about Dan and about seeing Joe in the coffee shop and about Chance. I just want to say his name. Drop it casually into conversation. But I don't say it. I feel stupid. I twist my knee around until it hurts and then bend over, to pretend to stretch. How long do I have to stand here? She stares at me, waiting for me to say something I guess. "Well," I say. I see her shivering, so I say, "I have to go."

"Okay," she says, and gives me a quick hug. She seems to be in a much better mood all of a sudden. "Okay, thanks for coming. You're really sweet."

"Whatever," I tell her. I'm backing away. I fight the urge to hurry. I can still see her sitting out there on the porch as I peddle away. My knee is swelling up. This probably wasn't a good idea. I am almost home when a police cruiser passes me and I almost fall off my bike trying to read the number: 6087. It's not him.

It's never him.

I don't know why I feel so disappointed.

Chance, I say to myself. *Joe*, says the echo inside me.

I leave my bike outside and go in, and the house is completely quiet. The door to Mom and Dad's room is shut, and I know what that means. I rush by it quickly to my own room, and try not to listen for those sounds. That's pretty disgusting. I guess they made up. I think of that slut secretary standing there in the front hall all flushed and happy and I just about throw up. Again.

In my room, I pull out an old album of pictures of me and Sam, growing up. Growing up might be the wrong expression. Sam didn't get to grow up, did he? I stay up late, looking at those pictures. I take them out of the album and press them up against my cheek and run my fingers along the sharp edges and breathe on them so that the shininess of them fogs up. In some of them, the colours are fading. I try really hard to remember everything that happened in each one, but I can't. I spread them out on my pillow and press my face on them, hoping to absorb them somehow. How could I be forgetting?

I dream about the mountain and the snow and the avalanche. I wake up screaming when I feel the rope snap. I scream and I scream, but no one comes to see if I'm all right. And I wonder if I really screamed out loud at all, or if it was all just in my own head.

I put the pictures back in the box, line them all up so their edges are straight. It takes a long time. The night leaks slowly out of the sky, and by the time I'm finished the sun is squinting into the blackness, a tiny rim of fire between the mountains across the Strait.

CHAPTER 9

I want to think the Prozac has made it better, that everything is better. There are no miracles, remember that. If there were miracles, Sam could have been saved. Sam could have been found and revived. Last winter, some kid wandered out into the snow and froze to death. Hours later, they thawed her out and she was fine. Completely normal. A miracle, the papers blazed.

Sam could be like that. Frozen. Suspended. That would be a fucking miracle, I think. That would be something to make headlines about.

I should have known better.

The thing is, that they find him. They find his body. I come home from school one day and there is a message on the answering machine from the police department in that community where the mountain was. I listen to the message and something falls inside me and falls and falls. There is no Prozac for that. There is no pill you can swallow that can do anything for that kind of falling.

I shake all over. The feathers fill me up and pour out of every pore. The feathers fill the house. I call Mom at work. I never do that. I give her the number to call. I guess she does. I guess some time passes. She comes home. She sits with me at the table and we don't say anything. Dad comes home.

There we are. The three of us.

"They're going to ship the body out here," Mom says. She chokes on the word body and starts to gag. I've never seen her like this.

"Thank God they found him," Dad says. "Now we can give him a proper burial."

I look at him. Proper burial. There is already a stone at the cemetery, marking the place where he would be if we had him. We're getting him back. I'm excited. I'm sick. I don't know what to think.

"Will we be able to see him?" I ask.

"No," Mom says abruptly. "There isn't anything to see."

"But," I say. I'm thinking of that frozen kid. Maybe …

"It's bones, Pagan," Dad says. "They used dental records …"

"Shut up," I say. "Shut the hell up. Shut up."

I try to move. Try to go upstairs. But I faint instead. A grey drop cloth covering up the kitchen light, the white counter. It's okay, though. I guess they carry me upstairs. I guess they put me to bed. I remember they give me something to swallow. A tranquillizer. I'm tranquil. I fall into a dream of whiteness.

The day we bury the body, the casket, it's raining. It's like something from a film. The ground behind the stone is open already, waiting. There is a minister and he says some stuff. No one is there except Mom and Dad and me. I have an umbrella but I don't open it. I want to get wet. I want to drown in it. The coffin is short. A child's coffin. I fight the urge to throw myself down on it. He isn't in there, I remind myself. He's gone. He's gone a long time ago.

Mom sobs through the whole thing. It's surreal, to see her cry. *Buck up, camper*, I want to say. *Tomorrow is another day*. I put my arm around her instead, and lean on her shoulder. She's shorter than me. When did that happen? There should be crows circling in the sky to complete the picture, but I look up and it's just rain, stinging my eye. Soaking my patch.

I get through it. We get through it.

I thought it would make things better. I can't believe it's real, that he's really in the ground.

Nothing changes. Except maybe that I slip back a step. My grief bubbles back up inside. I feel more like I'm faking, again. Less like I really care what goes on.

I should have known it was coming, I guess. I should have paid attention to the warnings. I should have known this grief was too big to be swallowed away with a capsule. Swallow, swallow, swallow. I should have listened. Dr. K. warned me about this. He gave me things to read, and although I didn't read them, I remember the word: burnout.

Burnout. It doesn't sound like enough of a word to describe what happens, or what happened next. It sounds almost gentle. A candle being snuffed out. A lightbulb fizzling and sinking into darkness.

It is going to be okay, I think. Everything is going to be okay. We buried him. It will be fine. I can get through it.

I go out with Chance a few times. I am dating. It's so normal that it curls my lip. It makes me wary. I am being a normal teenage girl. I pretend to be in love with him, because I want to be. I'm not. I know that. But he is so nice to me. I think, oh, something good is happening for me. We go to a movie and a couple of parties. We hold hands and he kisses me. Kissing him is like falling into a dream without being asleep. His lips make my legs give away. I kiss him sitting down, so I don't fall over. He wants more and more. Always more. I hardly know him. I just met him. I tell him that it's too soon. He has to wait.

I'm never going to sleep with him. I know that. That is something I'll never be ready for. I'm not that normal. There's only so much that Prozac can do. I'm not going to tell him that. I just want him to kiss me for a while longer. I want to be a part of this. He says that it's okay, that he'll wait for me to be ready. I just like holding his hand. His hands are really soft. It was a nice feeling, to be part of a couple. Part of something bigger than just me. We are Pagan and Chance. Chance and Pagan. We don't talk about Sam. We don't talk about anything. I don't want to talk. I want him to ask, but he won't. Why would he? I forget that by not telling him about Sam, I'm not telling him about me. I forget that he can't understand me unless he hears about Sam.

And then it happens.

It.

You're going to think it's stupid. What happens to me is nothing compared to Sam dying, or burying Sam. Nothing compares to that. And yet, in some ways, it's worse.

It's a week or so before Christmas. School is just

barely over for the year. It has turned really cold and every day it threatens to snow and then doesn't. The roads freeze into ice when it rains. The air buzzes with cold, like it's something alive. My hair is going crazy. I have to wear it in braids to try to control it but I refuse to cut it. I haven't cut it for years. The hair at the bottom is the same hair that I had when I was fourteen. I'm not doing it as a symbolic gesture or anything, at least I don't think so. I just can't stand the idea of cutting it off.

We are at a party at the same house where we met. Nathan's parents are away again. At first I thought he lived here alone, but then I realized that the basement part is his but his parents live upstairs. The party has burst past the edges of his suite and spilled over up into their territory. No one seems to care, least of all me.

We are all kidding around in the living room when the power goes out. It literally goes out with a bang. For a second there is silence, except for the screaming of the wind. I'm a little bit drunk, a little bit out of it. Enough so that it feels like a dream. Someone lights some candles. Someone says, "This house is probably full of ghosts." People are laughing, but to tell you the truth, it freaks me out.

Someone tells that stupid story about the guy and the girl trapped in their car, out of gas, and the guy with the hook for a hand trying to break in. It's a story I remember from when I was twelve, and it didn't scare me then. It does now. I am just about to sneak out, when there is a huge crash from the other room.

B-flat minor, I think. It's not a crash, it's a chord. Then a bunch of chords, not in sequence. A discordant mess. It sounds like someone is punching out the piano. We all run in there, but slowly. I mean, it's like one of those movies where you know you shouldn't go into the dark room, but you do, and then you all get chopped up with a chainsaw or something. Only that doesn't happen.

The piano is in the living room, in front of a window. Above it, there is a crystal chandelier. In the candle-light, the crystal looks like drops of falling water. If I weren't scared, I'd think it was beautiful. The keys on the piano are going down and no one is near it.

One girl screams. It could be me. Probably, it is.

Someone laughs. "Dude," says Nathan. "It's a player piano. The power going out must have tripped the switch."

I mean, of course that's what it is. Obviously. There aren't any ghosts. Ghosts don't exist. My hands are shaking like crazy and there is a creepy feeling in the back of my neck, like there are little currents running down my spine. How could it play with no power? Figure that out.

Sam. Sam, Sam, Sam, I think. Sam could make that happen.

Everyone else goes out of the room, all talking at once, except for one guy who has passed out on the couch. There is a pool of vomit on the floor beside him. I don't know who he is, but looking at him makes me feel sick. Who are these people? I think. Why am I here?

And then the piano plays again.

It does.

It plays for me. I can hear it. No one else even looks. Is it even playing? I definitely hear it. It's something more familiar this time. I know you think I'm making this up, and maybe I am. I've been drinking. I'm taking Prozac. I took something else, too, and I don't even know what it was.

"Sam?" I whisper, so no one can hear me. The music keeps going, and somehow I think that it makes sense, that it must be him.

The music stops. I sit on the piano bench and touch it with my fingers and it sort of feels like it is still humming. I close my eyes and picture Sam swimming to the shore of that mountain lake. I picture him climbing out. Still fourteen. Still a boy. I rest my fingers on the keys, but I don't play anything. I must be talking because the boy on the sofa sits up. He looks at me.

"Shut the hell up," he says, and then he flops back down and passes out again.

I guess I start to cry. I have been sitting here for a long time. Forever. I've forgotten how to move away. The lights come back on and people move around me, but I can't quite see them. They swirl around me like grass moving in the wind or something just out of reach. I sit and I sit. My hands are on the keys, the cool, soft keys. The silent keys.

Someone bumps into me. Hard. Spilling a sticky drink all over me, all over the piano. I watch the amber liquid pour between the keys and then I just stand up. It's over, I think. I get up to go find Chance to take me home because I am feeling so strange. I just want to go home to lie down. I want to go to bed.

I go into all these rooms, looking for him. The lights are back on, but it's still mostly dark. Maybe some light-bulbs blew out when the power surged, I don't know. I don't know how electricity works. It's hard to tell who is who without the lights. Everyone dresses so much alike, and I'm feeling so hazy. I grab one guy who is wearing a denim jacket like Chance's, but it isn't him. He tries to kiss me anyway. Who are these people, I think again.

"I have to go," I tell him. "Stop it, I have to go."

I'm running now. It feels like there are a million stairs in this house and I've gone up and down every one of them. I'm sweating when I get to this door at the end of the hall. It is the last place he could be, the only place I haven't looked. I think, maybe it's the bathroom, so I knock.

No one answers, so I go in.

And there they are. Obviously, obviously. Who do you think?

Brett and Chance.

I can't believe it. My feet are frozen to the floor. It's a dream, I tell myself. It's a dream. No, I'm saying that part out loud. Screaming. "It's a dream, it's a dream."

I'm screaming and screaming. Someone is holding my arms, but they don't need to, I'm not moving my arms, only my lips.

"Jesus, shut her up," someone says. Not someone. Chance. My Chance. Pagan and Chance.

"It's just a dream," I whisper. I say it over and over again. I'm crazy, I know it. But I can't stop. I say it and say it and say it. Red and blue lights flash outside, filling the shadows with light. I look out the window and see the police cars that have come to shut the party down.

It doesn't seem like something worth caring about. Brett and Chance jump out of the bed and put their clothes on and push past me like I'm not even there. They run down the stairs, buttoning their shirts. I just stand there, watching. When they are gone, I go over and sit on the bed. It is warm and smells bad, like mustiness and sweat and sex.

I feel so sick. I'm paralyzed. I swear that I can't move, I can't see, I can't hear. I feel the sheets and they are warm and sticky and I lie back in them.

It's just a dream. It's all a dream. Sam's bones in a box in the ground. Being normal. All a dream. The craziness is a tide that washes back out and carries me away. Just a dream, I say. All a dream.

In the doorway, a man is standing. Who is it? A policeman. Of course, of course. My parents are going to be so mad. My tongue is too big in my mouth to say anything.

"Come with me," he says.

But I can't. I'm stuck. I'm trapped. He grabs me and pulls me down the stairs. My knee screams, or I do. Or I don't. He drags me across the lawn. He thinks I'm drunk, I know he does. Maybe he isn't wrong. The back of his hand is covered with a smattering of black hair. His watch is gold. He puts me in the back seat of the car. The car: 888.

Oh God, I think, I can't do this, I can't. Joe. I duck low so he can't see me. I flip my hair forward and hide behind it. I don't want anyone to see me looking like this, much less Joe. Handsome Joe, my guardian angel.

"Sam," I say, "help me out here."

Joe gets into the car and slams the door. He doesn't even look at me. He doesn't say anything. His partner in the passenger seat turns around to look at me. He asks the questions. I can't answer. I just sit there and stare through my curtain of hair, stare at these men who can't help me. No one can help me.

Except Sam.

It gets worse, but I'm not paying attention so it makes things easier. I wait at the police station for Mom and Dad. Someone must have called them, must have got my ID from my wallet, or maybe I told them. I don't know. I follow them to their car, reminding myself how to walk, left right left right. Reminding myself to breathe, inhale exhale inhale exhale.

"What's wrong with you?" Mom keeps saying. "I don't understand. What's wrong with you? Please don't do this now. Please."

I can't answer her. I press my face against the cold glass of the window. It feels like the stars are flying through my brain. *I'm invisible, I don't exist, I've faded away to nothing.* Her words are just an echo: "What's wrong with you? What's wrong with *you?*"

"What's wrong with you?" I say. "What's wrong with you?"

I can't feel my hands. I think I'm crying, but not out loud, in my head. My face is wet.

Dad says, "We have to take her in."

Take me in, I think. *Yes, someone take me in.* Mom says, "No, it isn't that, she's drunk, that's all."

"That isn't all," Dad says. "Come on."

"I can't do it again," Mom says. "I don't think I can do it again, for Christ sake. I can't."

"Snap out of it," Dad says. "Pagan, we're taking you in."

"Okay," I say. "Okay, okay. Sorry, Mom. Sorry sorry sorry sorry sorry. Sorry Mom. Sorry Sam." I keep saying it. I chant. Sorry sorry sorry sorry.

Next thing I know, I'm in the hospital behind those old green curtains, waiting to see Dr. Killjoy. I've been here my whole life, I think. Everything else was just a dream. I've stopped apologizing. I'm letting Mom talk. I'm letting Dad answer. It's easier this way, and it's getting harder for me to concentrate. It's like I'm being pulled down and down and down into that dark, cold place and I can't be bothered to try to get out. I keep seeing Chance and Brett and that piano and Sam. Of course, Sam. I see him at the end of the rope, and then I feel the rope breaking, and I start crying again.

I see him, in the lake, eyes wide open, looking. Looking for me.

He was in the middle of a sentence when he fell. He never finished what he was going to say. He died when he was perfect. He never had a chance to screw up like me. He never had a chance to make mistakes, to make me hate him.

He would hate who I've become, my fingers stained yellow with nicotine, my friends not friends at all but just people who don't care enough to know me.

I guess they give me something to sedate me because I fall asleep. I really fall. Spiralling down and down and down into it. I always feel like I am always falling. The thing is, I'm pretty sure there's no one at the bottom to catch me.

Not this time.

I don't bother fighting it. I let the sleep take me, wherever it wants to go is probably better than here.

CHAPTER 10

I don't ever want to get out of bed. How long have I been here? I have been lying here forever. Growing up. I've spent my whole life in this bed. I'm at home. The curtains are closed, and only a small amount of light trickles in through the crack. It smells stale in here. It could be me. I haven't had a shower for a week, or more. I have no idea when my last shower was. I have no idea what day it is. I have no idea why I'm still alive and I don't care. Did I miss Christmas?

Who cares?

The lights are still up. Dad has hung them around my window. They flash red and green. They are on, so it must be evening. He has a timer that he sets so that they come on at five every day. I don't want to see them. Just the flickers I can see through the fabric of the drapes sets my teeth on edge. It makes me want to scream.

Christmas. It seems like such a strange, stupid, pointless idea. It's supposed to be about Jesus and God and all that, and instead it seems to be about buying a bunch of junk and wrapping it in expensive paper and having flashing lights all over your house. It's about remembering all the times that you loved Christmas and remembering that someone's dead and it will never be the same again. It's about death.

I am so goddamn angry. I want to stick pins through my skin. I want to cut deep with knives. I want to bruise and bleed.

I hate everything and everybody.

I wish I could go back to sleep, but I can't. I'll lie here awake until my body gives in and sleeps again. I hold my hand up in front of my face, and in the dim light I examine my lifeline. There is a scar that crosses over it, from the frostbite. It bisects the line perfectly like a line drawn with a ruler, an angle measured perfectly to make ninety degrees.

I think about Sam, just to think about something. Just to feel something. But I can't even work up that strong of a feeling about him. I just feel completely flat, like there is a layer of something thick and impenetrable between me and the rest of the world. A layer of mud or ice, or a glacier that is a million miles deep. In my bedside table drawer, I have a scalpel. I stole it from biology lab. It still has the smell of formaldehyde on it, even though I washed it with soap and water and ran boiling water on it. I don't know what I'm going to do with it, not at first. I guess in the back of my mind, I'm thinking of doing it again. It. The bathtub scene, the blood, the sliding away. Maybe.

But then another day goes by, and I don't.

I take it out of the drawer and look at it. It looks like a butter knife, but sharp. And small. I don't feel anything. I take the blade and press it gently into my thigh. The blood comes first, a tiny row of beaded redness. And then it hurts. It hurts and it hurts and it hurts, so I press a tissue down on it, hard, to stop the bleeding.

Hard enough to feel it hurt again and again.

I put the blade away. That's enough for now.

Sometimes Dan comes over and just stares at me. He doesn't say anything. Honestly, it makes me feel a little weird. Weirder than anything else, but good, in a way, because obviously he cares about me. Weird because of the silence. Weird because Sam isn't here with him. Weird because he is so obviously not fourteen anymore and Sam no longer exists and I am only half here. I think he's here every day. I can't keep track.

I guess Dan is living at his cousin's place. He looks different. He's either lost weight or gained it, or changed the way he dresses or does his hair. I can't quite pinpoint it, he just seems ... different. He's grown a bit of a beard. It makes him look even cuter than before.

"Girls must go crazy for him," Mom says, once, after he is gone.

I just shrug. I don't have the energy to explain it to her even if I could.

The walls sometimes close in on me. The ceiling is cracked and stained. It looks like a map, the cracks are rivers. Or maybe it looks like flesh, and the cracks are veins. When the curtains are open, I watch clouds and rain blow past. That's all I see from my spot in the bed. Dad comes in and brings me food and Mom ignores me, mostly, or pops her head in to say something that she learned in group. It's all garbage.

I have all my old pictures of Sam and me pinned to the wall, so the first thing I see in the morning is our matching gap-toothed grins on our seven-year-old faces.

I might never leave this room.

Brett hasn't called me at all; neither has Chance,

though I'm not that surprised about that. Nice friends I have, I think, bitterly. This never would have happened if Sam were still alive. We would still have the same friends that we always did: Dan and Trina and Ashley. We would still do good safe things like go to movies or go ice skating or to the mall. We wouldn't go to parties and take drugs and drink too much and sleep with each other's boyfriends.

God.

I hate him, I think. I hate him and I hate him and I hate him for leaving me alone. For leaving me with this.

"Fuck you, Sam," I whisper and I get out of bed. I take down the pictures. I take them all down and rip them up into smaller and smaller pieces. The Polaroids don't tear easily, and the sharp edges scratch my hands, but I can't stop.

I hate you, I hate you, I hate you, I say inside my head.

Dr. Killjoy wants me to start taking pills again, something different this time, and something that can't be mixed with alcohol or street drugs. Something he would monitor. Something I would have to be careful with. I tell him, "No."

I might never do anything again.

I fall asleep and I don't dream. There is just nothing, blackness, eternity. I am always disappointed to wake up.

It is New Year's Eve. I know this because Mom told me. She came in today and sat on the edge of my bed and said, "Are you going to get up and celebrate with us?" And I said, "No." And she said, "Pagan, would you please get up?"

I didn't say anything. Yes, I did. I said, "I'll try."

I've been lying here, deciding, ever since. The door opens. It's Dan. No one knocks. It's not like they are going to interrupt me, seeing as I'm not doing anything. He sits down next to me on my bed. He smells good. He must be nearly gagging on the smell of me. For a second, I feel a bit embarrassed.

"Hi," I say.

He looks at me. He is wearing sweats and has a bag of stuff in his hand. I watch him, half interested, as he unloads a bunch of clothes from the bag. New clothes. Girl's clothes.

"Get dressed," he says. Seeing as how this is the first thing he has said to me in two weeks, I do. I do it. I stink. I am really aware of that as he sits there and watches me. He's like a brother. I don't feel weird or anything getting changed in front of him.

My legs feel all wobbly like they do when you are recovering from a really bad case of the flu. They aren't connected. I am not connected to my body. My head is light and wispy, swaying on my neck like a helium balloon, barely attached. I tip and wobble and have to grab the wall for support. I try to glare at him, but he ignores me. He just steers me down the stairs and out the door.

It's freezing. Why is it always cold? I can't remember it ever being summer. I can't remember ever being hot. It is so cold that our breath travels with us, in front of us. I watch myself hyperventilate, build a bigger cloud. It must have snowed some time recently because there are patches of white on the lawns and small piles of it at the end of everyone's walkway. He has put our bikes out on the lawn, and he says, "Get on." No, I think. It's cold, I think. I can't, I think.

But I do. No one else ever tells me what to do, and I don't have the strength or energy to argue.

I get on and the bike swivels around under me. I push off from the curb and try to move my legs in a normal way. They feel stiff and creaky and don't seem to want to cooperate at all.

I fall off about a block away from home. It isn't a graceful fall, or a really dramatic one. I am just pedaling so slowly that the bike can't stay upright and over I go. The pavement is freezing. It doesn't hurt. It is cold like the surface of a Popsicle, the kind of dry cold you worry about sticking to forever. Luckily, I am wearing so many clothes that it doesn't really hurt, but it does knock the wind out of me. For a couple of long seconds I can't remember whether to breathe in or out and I just sit there on the freezing road and gasp.

Inhale, exhale, I think. Inhale, exhale. It takes me a minute to get it right.

"Get up," he says.

So I do.

I get up and we ride a little faster and then a little faster and finally we are going fast. We are cutting through the cold air like blades. It isn't snowing now, but it looks like it might. The sky is dark and heavy. We zoom past houses all lit up and trees decorated with flashing bulbs and living rooms crowded with people having small parties. We ride faster and faster and farther and farther, past everything to the beach and then we ride along the waterfront and breathe the salt air and the fresh wind. There are gulls circling way up high, trapped in the wind current, and there are people out walking their dogs. The waves are crashing in, heaving themselves up on to the road.

I can almost hear my body waking up as if from a really long sleep.

We ride for a couple of hours and then turn around and go home. I run right into the kitchen and drink three glasses of water. I feel like I've never had a drink before. My body was so dry. No wonder I couldn't move. I drink and drink, water spilling down over my chin. Dan leaves, still without saying anything.

I call out, "Thanks."

I hope he heard me.

I am just pouring one more glass of water when I see my bottle of pills on the counter, and I feel that jagged edge of fear rip through me like a current. And I remember: I'm not normal, I'm depressed, my brother died, I can't handle things.

It's like a flashbulb, remembering. I feel my knees buckling and I slide down to the floor. I can't get up. Really, I can't be bothered, or I just can't. I sit there and Mom comes in and starts baking cookies. For "group," no doubt. She ignores me, stepping over to get the flour, the eggs, the butter, the food coloring. The phone rings and she answers and has a long conversation with someone about someone else whom I have never even heard of, and it occurs to me, down there on the kitchen floor, that my mom has this whole life that I don't know about: friends I have never met, a job I don't understand, feelings I never even much considered.

I get up. I drag myself up by pulling on the kitchen cupboard door. The handle bends, but I don't care. I climb the stairs to my room. It seems like the longest staircase in the world, but I just was thinking that maybe I don't belong there on my mom's floor, in my mom's world. Maybe I don't fit in there at all. I had to get out of her way.

I try to get myself back. I have a shower and stare at myself in the mirror. If it weren't for the breasts and long hair, I could be Sam. No, no, I couldn't. I have a girl's face. Sam is disappearing from my features. He is. We buried him. Bones. I guess his teeth would have loosened and fallen out. I grin in the mirror and look at the gap. It's starting to close. My wisdom teeth are coming in and pushing my other teeth together. I pull my hair back and stare at my skin. If I could look beyond it, he'd be in me, looking out. He used to be. He can't be gone. I won't let it happen. I haven't finished yet. I haven't said good-bye.

The day after New Year's, I'm in Dr. Killjoy's office. I'm about three hours early, so I have to sit in the waiting room and stare at all the other pathetic people going in and out. This, in case you don't know, is the unwritten law of crazy patients: never arrive early. You are supposed to arrive exactly on time, and if you should happen to cross paths with someone who is leaving, you don't look at them. There is privacy in craziness. I break all the rules. I sit there and stare at the other patients and wonder what's wrong with them, and compare myself to them, and am basically rude. I pretend to read a magazine, but I am trying to listen through the thin walls to what Dr. Killjoy is saying to other people. See what wise things he has for everyone else that he doesn't have for me.

When it is finally my turn, I slump into my usual seat and glare at him until he says, "What's up, Pagan?"

And then I start to cry. I don't know if I have ever cried in his office before. Real crying, not just quiet tears. I blubber like a baby. I never have before. Not here. All those boxes of tissues made me not want to cry, they were so blatantly placed around the room. I thought it was sort of pathetic. But now, once I start, I can't stop, I just keep crying and crying and crying, and then I start talking: about Sam, about Dan, about Chance, about Brett, and finally, about me.

Me, me, me, I hear myself saying. Me.

I think I over-run my hour. It sure feels like a long time. A dozen buses have passed by and they only go by every fifteen minutes. I wonder if he's going to charge my parents extra for this. He doesn't say anything about it to me. He gives me a smile and a pat on the shoulder, and says, "You probably feel better already."

I nod, and then he passes me a prescription. He says, "I am adjusting your pills, and adding something new. For the short term. To help you through the tough bits."

God, I think. It's all a tough bit. Every day is a tough bit. Do I need another miracle? I don't think I can handle anything more. But still I take the piece of paper and go directly to the drugstore. I can't do this alone. My leg hurts still from where I dug into it with the blade. I can feel it when I walk, and it reminds me.

Eat me, drink me, swallow me. If he wants me to

swallow every pill in the pharmacy, I will. I'm just so tired of everything, tired of myself, even tired of Sam. I march right in to the store and pass the new magic prescription to the pharmacist and wait right there until he produces the bottles.

I go straight home and pop them and wait for things to settle down inside of me.

Ha.

While I'm waiting, I go sit at the piano. I don't play anything. I just sit there and wait to see if Sam is going to come and play for me. I wait to see if he is going to come back again.

I want to hear the piano, crashing and alive. I want to not be afraid.

I sit there until my butt starts to hurt and then I go into the kitchen and start making supper. I make spaghetti and meatballs and lay the table and when Mom and Dad arrive home, I serve them big heaping plates of rich pasta and I even clear the table and wash the dishes. I can't eat it myself. My stomach heaves and settles. I eat a salad of crunchy raw vegetables and lots of lettuce. My parents deserve better than that. I mean, they've probably had enough of me. I should try to give something back.

I don't feel any different when I go to bed that night, but I do change the sheets first. I mean, you can only sleep in a bed that stinks for a short while before it starts to be too disgusting.

CHAPTER 11

I ride my bike every day now, even though sometimes it is still slippery and icy. February is usually the worst month and it's just around the corner. Just when you think winter is over, it gets worse. It's not too bad this year, there isn't any further sign of snow. It threatened, and then it backed off. If I was still into skiing, I'd probably be disappointed. But that's the one thing that I'll never do again. Not without Sam. I don't know why all my memories of winter as a kid have snow in them. It doesn't snow here that often, even though it is Canada. It's a stereotype, that image of snow and sleddogs and all that other junk. It only snows in the mountains. That's the only snow that you can count on.

My mom bought me a new helmet. It's really nice. If you have to wear one, it might as well be cool. It's a late Christmas present. We did Christmas in January. I gave them books, because that's what Sam would have given them. Books and music. Even though he was an athletic kid, he was really into that kind of stuff, too. It's funny, I'm starting to remember him as a *kid*, as some kid I used to know.

He never got to be my age.

Always, before, I would think of him being the same as me, but now I am remembering him as a different person. It's scary, to tell you the truth. It scares me to think of him as a stranger, as someone separate from me.

After hours of arguing, my parents give in and agree to not celebrate my birthday. What's to celebrate? It passes by like any other day. It's meaningless. I sit in my room and look at pictures of Sam.

It rains.

I sit out on the roof and get soaked. I can't light my cigarette. The rain keeps putting out the flame.

I'm starting to vary my bike route every day. I ride through parts of the city that I've never had any reason to be in before. Sometimes Dan comes with me, but not too much. He moved back in with his parents again, right on New Year's Day. He says it's pretty weird, everyone is acting super-polite. I think his dad is in therapy. Well, if anyone needs it, it's him. I hope he's taking Prozac. So, needless to say, Dan doesn't have that much time for me right now.

It's okay. I like riding alone. I ride through all these residential areas, some of them really ritzy and some of them much more shabby. I look into windows as I ride by and imagine what each life must be like in each house. I pick out my favourite houses — all with a view of the ocean — and the houses I would least like to own. Sometimes I pass by houses for sale that are open for viewing, and I take of my cycling shoes and go inside. I'm a really good liar. If I could steal a house, I probably would. I look at other people's stuff and their pictures on the mantle and the books they have on the shelf. That's one of my favourite things to do. I meet realtors. The probably know my dad. Do they know who I am? I make up names. Peggy Samuels, I say. Patty Daniels. I tell them that my family is thinking of moving, and I am just scouting out houses while I am waiting for them to come from out-of-town. I make up this whole story about how I am going to school here and living with my grandmother in an apartment downtown. I don't really have a grandma, but when I say that I do I can describe her. I see her clearly, her stooped back and long silver hair. The laugh lines around her eyes and mouth. The dentures she keeps in a cup on her bedside table. The way she knits sweaters.

"She knit me this sweater," I say, tugging at my designer top. "She sewed these pants."

Lie, lie, lie. I tell them I have a brother. I tell them he's a twin. I roll my eyes when I describe him. I say, we need a room in the basement for him. He's wild. I can't help it. I can't stop. We have a dog, I say. A golden retriever. We have two cats, I tell them. We have a tropical fish tank that holds a hundred gallons of water and a thousand coloured fish. We need a yard big enough to build a pool, I say. I'm a swimmer. I flex my muscles. I show them that I'm strong.

They don't care. They show me around like I'm someone real. Someone who could buy their house. I take their leaflets, floor plans, business cards. I put them in the pile of papers on my desk, the growing pile.

I took some extra time off school. I got an extended winter break, really. My doctor wrote me a note. I want to know what it said. I can't imagine what he wrote. "Please excuse Pagan from January. She was crazy. She couldn't get out of bed."

I have to go back to school on Monday. On my last free day I ride all over the place, from one end of the city to the other. I ride to the pool and swim laps. I swim for hours. The chlorinated water skims off my body. I'm a dolphin, a fish, a whale. I do a hundred laps. My arms protest and burn.

I get back on my bike and ride. I haven't eaten anything. I'm weightless. That's when I see Joe. He is standing on the sidewalk outside this house. He isn't wearing his uniform, but I know it's him. His pants are creased khakis. A denim shirt. My heart stops completely and I gasp for air. How does he do this to me? The house is small and grey with a white trim and a thick green hedge. It even has this little white picket fence and a tiny gate. It's almost too perfect, if you know what I mean. It's decorated up with white and blue lights that flash in sequence. None of them are burnt out. You can tell a lot about a family by the condition of their Christmas lights.

Of course you can also tell a lot about a family that still has their lights up at the end of January.

I remember that first time I saw Joe, and the message he had to deliver then. This time, he's just standing there. He pulls back his sleeve and looks at his watch. He's waiting, obviously. I ride by slowly, wondering if I can stop and talk to him, if he even remembers me. He puts up his hand and waves.

I stop and rest my foot on the curb. "Hi, " I say. "It's Joe, right?" Like I'd ever be able to forget. Like I don't sometimes dream about him at night. In my dreams, he holds my hand. In my dreams, I walk beside him. We never kiss. Nothing like that. In my dreams, he glows with a soft white light.

And he says, "Pagan, how are you? Fallen off that thing lately?"

I laugh and say, "Nope, not lately."

I want it to be magic, like that first time, so I just stare at him. He shifts back and forth. "So," he says.

"So," I say.

If he's waiting, he's obviously waiting for someone. A woman comes out of the house. She puts her purse down and fidgets with her keys with one hand. There is something in her other hand. A baby. She's pretty, with long brown hair that is all curly and flowing down her back and she is wearing a velvet dress and high heels and is carrying a baby wrapped in a blue blanket. She's going to be cold, I think, then I do a double take. A baby. My heart beats wildly and I say, "Who's that?" I try to keep my tone light, hoping he is going to say his sister or his cousin.

"My wife," he says, "My wife and my baby boy, Sam."

"Oh," I say, and I feel tears stinging my eyes, which is really stupid. I mean, it's not like he could be interested in me anyway. Why would he be? I'm just an uncoordinated kid who fell off my bike one day and then went crazy at a party. That's all. He probably thinks I'm a freak with my eye patch and stringy hair and obvious craziness. The craziness that hovers over me like a flock of birds with invisible wings.

I tell him: "Sam was my brother's name. He died." And then I get on my bike and ride like mad down the street, my bike weaving underneath me as if it has to try really hard to keep up with my pumping legs.

I will always be alone. That's the thing, after Sam died, that was the worst. I was so lonely for him, all the time. I was left alone.

He left me all alone.

I'm not totally alone.

I have friends.

No, that isn't true either.

I see Brett at school on my very first day back, and she does-n't even talk to me. I can't believe it. She just glances at me and then walks right by, as though I was the one who needed to apologize. Fuck her. As much as I thought I liked her, I don't even think I knew her. I sure don't need her.

One of the first rumours that I hear when I go back to school is that Daisy isn't her sister at all, but her baby that she had when she was fourteen. If I heard that a month ago, I would have defended her to death, but now I don't know. It actually sort of fits. I think Brett might even be a little bit more lost than I am, but I can't help her. I mean, let's face it, I can barely help myself.

First thing I do is go to the guidance counsellor and say, "Look, I can't do *everything* anymore, I have to quit some stuff." This was Dr. Killjoy's idea. This is one of his suggestions that I have decided to agree with.

And she says, "Like what?" She sits there and twid-dles with her pen. She spins it on her finger. She's good at it. She doesn't drop it. It's one of those clear plastic pens, cheap, that you can buy for a quarter. She sighs. "Well?"

I think about it and I say, "I think I will keep up with swimming but no other teams. I just can't do it. I'm too tired. I just can't."

She says, "Well, Pagan, you're not a superhero, you don't have to do everything. Swimming is just great. And," she says, "I have some scholarship applications for you to fill out for college. You should try music and swimming. You're good enough at both to try for scholarships."

That gets me thinking about music. I mean, music was Sam's thing. Not really mine. I could play, but he's the one that really cared about it. I sit there for a minute and stare out her window into the parking lot. I can hear the clock ticking really loudly on the wall, like all clocks seem to do in school buildings. I can hear all the other students moving through the hallway between classes. Just at that moment, I imagine that I see the first flakes of snow falling.

"Wow," I say. "It's snowing."

"Oh," she says, and sighs. Again.

Her hair is the same flat grey colour as the sky, and there is some red lipstick on her front teeth. She obviously isn't someone who loves snow. Not like Sam and me. I imagine that she is thinking about driving in the snow, and all the work of shovelling the driveway and clearing the walk. I don't trust people who don't like snow. I, of all people, have a reason to not like it, but I still do. It reminds me of Sam.

She looks out the window. "That's not snow," she says. "Thank God."

"Yes, it is," I say, surprised, and look again. No, she's right. It's rain. Loosely falling.

"You know," I tell her, "I think I might not want to

use the music. I mean, I don't even know if I want to go to college."

"Oh," she says. "Okay, Pagan, whatever you want to do is fine. Just fill out the applications, though. You don't want to change your mind and have it be too late, right?"

"Right," I say.

"It's your choice," she says.

Which is true, I think, as I walk out of her office and get swallowed up by the river of kids. I can do anything I want. I don't have to decide right now. I don't have to be in a hurry. But I have to cover all the bases. Just in case.

At lunch, I find Dan. We go to the cafeteria and I say, "So, how's it going?"

"Okay," he says. But he looks tired and sad, and I say, "How's your Dad?"

"He left," he says. "He left."

"He left?" I repeat.

"Yeah," he says. "I should never have said anything. I ruined everything. I mean ... my mom ... "

"He left?" I repeat again. I think of my own crazy family and wonder if that could happen. I mean, my dad fooled around and my mom didn't leave. But still. I mean, it could happen to anyone, right? And I sure haven't made it easy for them. Besides, I read somewhere that when a child dies, the parents almost always split up. I shudder.

"It's my fault," he says, miserably. "You were right."

"No, I wasn't," I tell him. "I'm almost never right. Really."

"You were right," he says again.

Privately, I think that in his situation, it might not be such a bad thing that his dad left. I always thought that maybe his dad used to hit his mom and maybe that's what made Dan gay. That's a stupid thing to say, isn't it? It's a stupid thing to even think, I guess. But I thought maybe he was just looking for a man who could love him back, like his father never did.

Never mind.

He's gay because he is, and that's all there is to it. Things might get better with his dad gone.

I don't say any of that, I just lean on his shoulder and say, "Shit happens, huh."

And he smiles at me, but doesn't laugh. And that's that. Some of his football buddies come over and start chucking chips around and flirting with me, and I, for once, flirt back. Why not? I flirt back and pretend to be normal and for a whole hour, I don't think about Sam one time. Except to notice that I'm not thinking about him. I get to thinking about that Prozac dog, and his bone, and about how he just walked away and left it there. He didn't even look at it.

I stand up so fast that I knock over my plastic chair. I don't say anything, I just walk away from Dan and his friends. I just leave. I get my bike and ride around. I ride in the rain. It's pretty. Rain doesn't bother me. I picture it turning into snow. Big, fat flakes that stick to everything. I ride through a park and I see the flash of a deer, disappearing into the bush.

That afternoon, at Dr. Killian's office, we talk about how I always feel like I am not quite present, like I'm always on the outside looking in. He calms me down with his quiet, soothing voice. I tell him that I'm taking my pills, but that I hope I don't have to take them forever. I mean, they seem to be working, but who wants to be attached to a bottle of pills for the rest of their lives? I don't want them to be my secret to living a normal life.

I just want to be normal. I just want to move on.

I do. It's the truth, this time.

I fill out the applications. One, then two, then a third one. It gets easier. Write an essay, they say, about why you want to go to college. What you want to do. I want to be normal, I write. I want to be normal. I want to go to your college. I want to do the right thing.

I write until my hand cramps, until I can't see what I'm writing, but the pages fill and fill and the envelopes are full, stuffed with my words that I don't remember writing and my thoughts that I don't remember thinking. I stuff them in my bag. The school mails them for us. I've done my part. That's all I have to do. It's all I can do.

spring

CHAPTER 12

Look at me. I'm normal. I look in the mirror. My image smirks back.

Not normal, it says to me. *You're kidding yourself.*

I still my hands from shaking. I look at myself again. Fine, I say. I'm fine. It's Sunday morning. I am getting ready for a bike ride that I am going on with some of Dan's football friends. I might think they are jerks, but I've decided to give them a chance. Why not? It's the first time in a long time that I have gone out with anyone at all, except Dan. I am nervous and kind of excited. It's March. The weather is starting to break. Daffodils are up. It all seems hopeful.

I'm terrified. I take an extra pill. Not Prozac, something else. The emergency extra that Dr. K. gave me. It blurs the edges. Softens the colours.

I'm okay, I say to myself. I brush my teeth. I get dressed.

Sometimes it happens that we get a little flash of spring in February, before it gets cold again, and that's what happened this year. Now, it seems like it might even stick. The purple crocuses have pushed through the lawn and the sky is blue in that far away, pale way of a clear day in winter. I am in the kitchen putting my water bottle in the freezer when Mom and Dad come in, all dressed up.

"What are you doing?" I ask.

"What do you mean?" they say, together.

"Well, why are you all dressed up?"

"We're going to church, Pagan," Dad says. "We always go to church on Sunday. You just don't usually notice because you're out on your bike all day."

"Oh," I say. Did I know this? Maybe I did. I don't know what I know anymore. On Sunday I do stay away. Family stuff sometimes makes me too sad. I can't explain it.

"We've been going for a couple of months," Mom says, glancing at my dad. "You know that."

"Right," I say. "I just forgot. I just wasn't thinking."

Their new shoes squeak on the floor. The screen door springs shut behind them. Dad's hand rests on her waist. He opens the car door for her. I watch them drive out the driveway and think to myself, church? Did I know?

I feel like I've forgotten a lot of things. Like I've slept too much and wiped the slate clean.

His hand on her waist. I guess that means Dad isn't see-ing his secretary anymore. I think the church might frown on that. Adultery is one of the seven deadly sins, isn't it? Did he mention he had a new secretary? I don't remem-ber. If he said it, I wasn't listening. I don't even know what kind of church they are going to. I mean, it could be some-thing weird, like numerology or Satanism or something. It gives me the creeps. Maybe they roll around and speak in tongues. Nothing would surprise me anymore.

The only time I have ever been in a church was for Sam's funeral. I don't remember much of it. I was still pretty banged up. I was even in a wheelchair, all dressed in black, with a scarf wrapped over my mangled eye. It was silk. I remember a bunch of hymns and prayers. People went up and said stuff about Sam, stuff they remembered. They told stories. I stared up at the stained glass with my good eye and tried to imagine myself somewhere else. I made up a city at the bottom of the lake, where Sam and I could live together. I imagined we could breathe underwater.

Our piano teacher got so emotional she had to stop in the middle of what she was saying and go sit down. Someone sang a really pretty song, I remember that. I sort of listened to that. Dan threw up on Dad's shoes.

Afterwards, Dad was mad about the prayers they said because he said they were meaningless. He said that if there was a God, he wouldn't have taken Sam away from us like that. I always thought that was true, too. What kind of God would do that?

I guess I'm kind of curious about where they went and what made them change their mind. Their secret life. Without me.

I have to go. I have a bike ride to go on.

We drive out to the park in a van that belongs to someone's parents. It smells new and expensive. Leather seats that heat up at the touch of a button. I feel kind of bad about piling all our dirty old bikes in the back. Hunks of mud and stuff drop down onto the floor. The kid who's driving is Robert, I think, but for some reason, they call him Boob. I guess it's some kind of play on "Bob." It's hard to take a guy named Boob very seriously, but he's funny, so I don't have to try too hard. I get to sit up front with him because I'm the girl. He sings along to the songs on the radio — which plays so loudly that the whole van vibrates — but he mixes the words up on purpose, so he is singing about "hamburgers and fries" instead of "her beautiful eyes." Stuff like that. Normal stuff. The pill is working. I feel sleepy and happy. He makes me feel less nervous. For a little while, I was feeling scared. What if I had a panic attack? What if I made a fool of myself? At the last minute, Dan had to back out, so there is really no one here that I know. What would they think of me if I suddenly collapsed or starting crying and couldn't stop? Boob is a good distraction. I laugh at his jokes and actually start singing along a little bit. I have a terrible singing voice. It was Sam who got that gift, not me. He could sing like an angel.

After about an hour of driving, we get there. We load the stuff out of the car and onto the trails. It's pretty cold, but it's a beautiful day and we can hear birds calling. It's really really quiet out here. It's some kind of bird sanctuary park, so there are signs that talk about the different kinds of birds that we might see. No one reads them, but I'm kind of interested, so I look at them while I'm pretending to fix the seat of my bike.

I haven't been riding on trails since Sam died. It takes me a few minutes of pedalling to remember all that stuff about jumping over tree roots and climbing over logs and how slippery gravel can be. We ride for a while on relatively easy paths and I don't fall off. I feel pretty good. I'm wearing sunglasses instead of the patch, so I imagine that I look pretty normal. Just a normal girl out for a ride with a bunch of good-looking guys. That's a normal thing to do, right? I pull my hair back into a braid so that it doesn't flap around my face, and I can feel the cool wind blowing on my neck. It's a very peaceful feeling.

One of the guys, Caleb is his name — he's this big tough guy who is the all-star quarterback on Dan's football team — he says, "This is girly stuff, let's get going." He looks right at me and says, "That is, if you can handle it."

I get all defensive and say, "Of course I can."

He reminded me of Sam when he said that. Sam always did stuff like that to challenge me. He knew that I'd never back away from a challenge.

We ride straight up this steep hill and stop at the top. It's beautiful up there. You can see the whole city in the distance. It seems really far away. The funny thing is that the height doesn't really bother me. I thought it might. I haven't been up a mountain since. Well. You know.

I thought it would bother me. It doesn't. I feel okay. I feel like I fit in. We are all quiet, except for the sounds of all of us breathing hard from the ride up.

Caleb says, "Now, for the good part!"

And they start yahooing and yippeeing and next thing I know, they are riding over the edge of what looks to be a cliff. Well, I think to myself, if they can do it, I can do it. I push off and follow them and get about half way down when my bike starts going one way and I start going the other way. The sky skids out of sight in a blur of dirt and branches. Next thing I know I am hanging over the edge of nothingness with my foot stuck in my pedal and my bike stuck on a root. All I can see is ... nothing. Just a steep drop-off and then a river about a million miles below me.

I think: Great, now I am going to die by falling off a

mountain, too.

I think: Mom and Dad are pretty much going to have to stop believing in God now. I'm not really scared, even though I can feel my heart beating fast and I am breathing hard from the exertion of not falling. I am just dangling there, waiting for someone to notice I am missing. A seagull flies by right at my level, and seems to stop as if to say, "What are you doing?" That's when I start laughing. The laughing jiggles the bike, and I am just hanging there laughing when I hear a voice saying, "Holy shit!"

I look up and there is Boob. He is pulling my bike up and reaching out his hand to rescue me. I try to stop laughing so that I have some strength in my arm to help pull myself to safety.

"Wow," he says. "That was close, are you okay?"

"Actually," I say, "I feel pretty good." I grab my bike from him and take off. I just fly down the rest of that mountain. I'm not afraid of anything. I can feel rocks and roots and branches underneath me and my bike behaves like a live animal, reacting to everything and I make it all the way down without falling again.

The next day at school, Dan is looking at me funny. "What's wrong with you?" I say.

And he says, "I don't know, I think ..."

And I say, "What?"

"Robert likes you," he says, blushing.

"Who?" I say.

"Robert. You know," he pauses, "Boob."

"You're kidding," I laugh. "Boob?"

"Yeah," he says, and starts twiddling with his laces.

Then I realize something. "Oh no," I say, "You don't have a thing for him, do you?"

He shrugs. "Forget it," he says. "He's straight."

I laugh again. "Well, don't worry," I tell him, "he's not my type."

Then I start wondering: Who is? What exactly is my type? Do I have a type? Joe and Joe and Joe.

Joe with his wife and baby.

In English class, I pretend to be listening to some kids reading out loud from Shakespeare, but what I am really doing is studying Boob out of the corner of my eye. I guess he's pretty cute. He's just so young. Young-looking. I mean, I know he's the same age as me.

Not like Chance, who is out of school already.

Not like Joe, who is so much a grown man.

I sort of drift off. I start thinking about Joe and imagining myself coming down the steps of his house with the baby in my arms. I imagine him looking at me the way he looked at that woman and saying, softly, "That's my wife."

I forget all about Boob after that. He's just a boy. A cute boy, but a boy after all.

On Saturday, it starts to rain. In some ways, March and April are the dreariest months of the year, the months when it rains and rains and rains and doesn't quit. I had swim practice early in the morning and my hair smells like chlorine. My swim times are getting better. I think it's because of the Prozac. I guess it's because of the Prozac. Without Prozac, I just sit and do nothing, so I'm grateful for it. I'm not scared of it anymore. I've stopped taking the Ativan, that was the other drug Dr. K. gave me. It made me sleepy. It made my dreams too bright, like the contrast on the TV was turned up too much, and I'd wake up feeling dazzled and afraid.

I'm sitting at the kitchen table daydreaming. Dr. Killian says I can start cutting back on the Prozac if I want to, but I sort of like this state I'm in. Just now, I've found a balance. I've been thinking about Joe, a lot. Obsessively. I keep thinking about the number on his car, 888, and about how his baby is named Sam. It seems like fate to me. I don't believe in a whole lot of things these days, but I do believe in fate, a little bit. I think that maybe Joe and I were meant to be together. That first time I met him, when he drove me home, it was like the air was humming with electricity. I swear it.

Maybe his wife is going to die. Maybe she has a cancer that's already started. Maybe it's just a matter of time.

I swallow sharply, tasting bile. What am I thinking?

I'm a monster. I push back from the table and grab my helmet. I hardly know what I'm doing, but I get on my bike and ride through the rain over to his house. What am I doing, I think. What am I doing here? But it doesn't stop me. I coast to a stop and I stand on the sidewalk with my bike for a long time. I love the smell of wet pavement and the green smell of wet grass. I feel pretty tired. It was a long ride. I'm winded. I stand there and stare and stare and finally his wife comes out and says, "Can I help you? Are you all right? Are you lost?"

I say, "I'm looking for Joe."

"Joe?" she says. "My husband isn't here right now."

The way she says "my husband" sounds so proprietary, so bossy and cold. I shiver. "I just was in the neighbourhood," I say. "Tell him I stopped by."

"Oh," she says, "are you a friend of his?" Her hair is pulled back under a scarf, and she looks frumpier than I remember. And older. But not like she's dying. Not like she's leaving.

"You could say that," I tell her. I kind of smile. I don't know why I'm doing that. It's more like a smirk. "You could say we're friends." My heart is beating like crazy. I guess it's from the riding. I can tell I'm blushing, my face is boiling hot. She kind of winces, like I've struck her and she says, "What's your name?"

"Pagan," I tell her. "Tell him Pagan came by."

I ride away fast before I can apologize to her. Before I can start feeling sorry for her. I mean, she's going to get hurt sooner or later when Joe realizes that we are meant to be together. All week, I kind of float along, thinking about Joe and imagining our life together. What am I doing this for? Am I crazy? I don't feel crazy. I don't. I've been crazy, so I sure know what to look out for. Instead, all of what I'm doing seems like the most obvious thing in the world.

It's Saturday. Early. I don't have any plans. At breakfast, I eat the pancakes that my mom makes and I help her with the dishes. I think we've reached a silent agreement. We don't say a lot, but we understand each other. At least, I think we do.

"Where are you going today?" she says.

"Nowhere," I say. But I say it nicely, not like I'm being rude. I am going nowhere. That's all I ever do.

No, that's a lie. I'm going to Joe's. It takes half an hour to ride to his house, half an hour of long, uphill stretches. I slow down a few blocks away and get my breath, smooth out my hair and wipe the sweat off my brow. Joe is in the yard, smoking a cigarette. Like it was meant to be this way. He smokes the way movie stars do, holding the cigarette between his thumb and his middle finger. The smoke curls up around his face like a halo when he exhales. I can see that he has a cut on his cheek from shaving and he has stuck a piece of tissue on it. I almost reach out and touch it, but I don't. He is leaning on a shovel, but he isn't really doing anything with it. He has started to dig a hole, but it looks like he hit a rock or something and gave up. His face is dirty and sweaty and I can feel my knees weaken.

"Hey," I say and stop and lean my bike against the fence.

"Pagan," he says. His voice is kind of flat and weird.

"What's up?" I say.

"You tell me," he says. "Just in the neighbourhood?"

"What?" I say.

"Pagan," he says, "I really like you." He stops and stares at me. I'm wearing my patch, and he stares at it for a minute, like he's looking for what it's hiding. I am just about to say, I like you, too, when he continues. "... And I might be way out of line here, but I think something is going on with you. My wife says ..."

"Excuse me?" I say. I try to pretend that I'm not dying, that I'm not completely humiliated. My hands are shaking. That hasn't happened for a long time, the shaking. I grip my handlebar hard to try to get them to stop. "I was just riding by ..."

"Pagan," he says, gently, but stern at the same time. "I'm happily married and you are way too young for me. Do you get it?"

"Yeah," I say, and push off from the fence. I'm freezing because I'm wearing these little shorts that make my legs look really long. I feel like an idiot. For a second, I think about killing myself. I think, I could just die right now. Then I realize, I don't mean it. I don't actually want to die anymore. I can't imagine doing it. I used to be able to imagine it easily. More easily than I could imagine living. I push the pedals down hard, so hard my legs ache and my knee hurts a bit from where I damaged it last year. I'm riding fast now, praying I don't fall off.

I can't believe I thought … I can't believe I'm so stupid … Oh, God.

"I won't bother you again," I say, but I'm way too far away for him to have heard me. I'm riding down a street I've never been on before. Riding hard, only half looking out for stop signs. There is a humming in my ears. I'm so embarrassed. I should have known. Why would he want to be with me?

I'm so stupid. I don't know how to read people. I thought I was so smart. I don't know anything.

When I get home, I'm sweaty and hot but the air is chilly so I'm shivering. I go upstairs and lie in the bathtub for a long time. In hot water, my scars turn purple. I can't even remember doing that. Making the cuts. It's like I'm remembering something I read, or something someone told me. I don't much remember being there. The water steams and my skin turns red. Under the water, I can see my breasts, the hair that has grown between my legs. I can see my changes. I push down on my hip bones and cover my breasts with my hands.

My body embarrasses me. I'm still not bleeding, not menstruating. I had one period, right before the accident. One night, I woke up and the sheets were stained with my blood and for a minute I thought I was dying and then I realized what it was. I remember having cramps, deep gut-piercing pains that I couldn't describe. I remember how I made Mom promise not to tell Sam. I didn't want him to know. I didn't want to change and become different from him.

Well, I'm different now, aren't I?

I pour in all these bath things that Mom has lying around, bubbles and oil and foam and I add more water so it froths up and blankets me. I'm invisible. The room stinks like rotting flowers. I don't care. I watch the steam rise and gradually fog over the mirror and the window and I lie there until the water gets cool and then cold, and my skin puckers up like an old raisin.

I wonder what Mom thinks when I stay in here this long. I wonder if she's hovering outside the door, scared to knock, waiting to hear a splash or a cough or anything to indicate I'm still alive.

At dinnertime my parents are acting all weird. They have laid out all the good china and stuff and my dad has made this elaborate prime rib dinner and they have a bottle of champagne in a bucket of ice. I don't like prime rib that much. I don't like how the meat looks like flesh, bloody and half alive. It makes me gag.

"What's going on?" I ask, yawning. All that biking and then the hot bath made me sleepy and I am beginning to get that familiar craving for my warm flannel sheets and an endless, dreamless sleep. I'm thinking that maybe I'll go to the music room after dinner and see if I can get Sam to play something. Just the idea of that makes the hair on the back of my neck stand up. I get goose bumps. I mean, if Sam can communicate with me through music, maybe he'll try again.

Maybe.

Maybe at the party he was there and trying to warn me about my so-called friends.

Maybe it wasn't just drugs and drinking. Maybe it was real.

"Your father and I have an announcement," Mom says, startling me out of my own head. For one heart-stopping moment I imagine she is going to say they have decided, finally, to split up. Instead she says, "We're getting married. Well, we wanted to ask you."

"What?" I say. "What? Ask me what? Get married. What does it have to do with me?"

"Oh, Pagan," she says. Her eyes fill up. I wonder how much I've made her cry in the last three years, how many gallons of tears she has spilled for me.

"We're going to get married," Dad says. "We're asking you to be a family with us."

"What were we before?" I say, suspiciously.

"We were lost," he tells me. "We were lost, but now we've found the way."

"Oh God," I say. "Great. Whatever." I feel queasy, looking at them. What have I not noticed? They went to church, sure. I thought they were praying for me, or praying for Sam or something. I don't know what I thought. I've never thought of them as a separate thing unto themselves before. I sit down and help myself to a big hunk of meat and potatoes and start eating like I've never seen food before. I haven't eaten meat for years. It sticks in my throat, but I swallow and swallow and swallow.

CHAPTER 13

The sun feels nearly hot on my skin. It isn't dark in the morning when I ride to school now, it's light and warm. The air itself feels less dense and easier to move through. My legs are strong from riding all winter and all spring. I measure the change of the season by the change in my strength. I'm stronger now. In a lot of ways.

School is winding down for the year. Forever, I guess. This is it. The last month. I can't believe I'm going to graduate, I can't believe I got into a college, whether I meant to or not. College. Graduation. Everything is changing, but instead of feeling afraid all the time, I feel almost hopeful. Still cautiously optimistic, I tell Dr. Killjoy. But the truth is, I'm still waiting for the other shoe to fall.

That doesn't mean I'm ever going back to where I was. This is a whole different feeling. More like anticipation. Dr. Killjoy thinks that it's the pills, of course. I stopped taking Prozac and switched to Paxil, which makes me feel less hyped up and edgy. They're all the same, I guess, or maybe they are all different. On Paxil, I feel more like me. Dr. Killjoy says the pills do different things to different people, and that sometimes one works better than another. I nod and agree with him, but part of me thinks that things are better because of the season. Because of the sun.

Also, now that I'm not doing so much music and sports and obsessing, I have more time to think about things. I've decided that I'm going to write in a journal everything that I remember about Sam. So far, all I've got is my very first memory ever.

We were about eighteen months old, and we were in our cribs in our bedroom. Our room was painted yellow, I remember, and it had a linoleum floor. I remember so clearly that there was this moment when we looked at each other and decided we were going to climb out of our cribs. That was enough of bars keeping us in. I don't think we could talk yet, but Sam and I never needed to do much talking. We just looked at each other and we knew. I remember piling up the toys and pillows and climbing up over the edge and falling on the floor, which was hard and cold. I knew I couldn't cry, because then we'd get caught. We'd get in trouble. I toddled over to Sam's crib and I helped him over so he wouldn't fall. I remember helping him. We went over into the corner and sat down in a little patch of sunlight that was coming in the window, and when Mom came in, we were asleep. I remember she said, "How on earth ... that's impossible!" The very next day, we got proper beds.

I wrote all that in my journal, along with all the details I could think of. Sam's blue pajamas with the train on them and the little gold flecks in the linoleum floor and the blue teddy bear I used as a step to climb out. Now that it's down on paper, I don't have to hold on to it so tightly. I was holding on to Sam like he was sand running through the cracks in my fists and I was panicking because he was slipping away.

It's that simple, and yet it's not.

I'm going to write everything I can remember. In case I ever start to forget. I still want to look back and relive every moment we had together.

I still feel sad, but in a less lonely way.

I look in the mirror and see myself. I have to look really hard to see Sam. I'm feeling better. I don't want to admit it to anyone, in case it goes away, this normal feeling. This feeling like I'm not going to fly off the earth and disappear like a wisp of smoke.

I'm standing at my locker, deciding if I'm going to go to math or if I'm going to cut it and go for a ride instead. It's such a nice day. Puffy white clouds in a blue sky. The air in the school is stale and old. Year end smell. Too much chalk dust in the ventilation system. Not enough open windows. I'm trying to decide what to do when I notice someone standing behind me. I have my bike gloves in my hand.

"I was wondering," Boob says, looking at the locker behind me over my right shoulder. "I was thinking ..."

"What's up, Boob?" I say.

"I was going to ..."

"Spit it out!" I tell him. I hate it when people start sentences and then don't finish them. He's blushing. He looks into my eye and I look away. Tap the patch with my gloved hand. The velcro sticks for a second. He waits for it to come unhitched. He looks away. He's waiting. I try to be a little kinder. "What did you want to ask, Boob?"

"Um, would you go to the dance with me?" He looks like he's in pain.

I'm really surprised he would ask me. I wasn't going to go to the dance. Dances are for other people. Normal people. It didn't even occur to me to go. I don't know how to dance. Not really. Not the way other people do. I stare at him and don't answer. He blinks rapidly. He has a nice face, I think. Gentle. My heart is beating strangely. I clear my throat. Feathers, I think. No, I think.

"Um," I say.

Since that bike ride, I've hardly even seen Boob. We aren't friends. It isn't like that. I look down the hallway. People are disappearing into classrooms. The open classroom doors suck them in like a sponge.

"The dance," I say.

I've been pretty busy helping Mom to plan the wedding. I mean, she's counting on me. I'm really involved. It's not really a wedding. More of a ceremony, like a graduation ceremony. Like our family graduated from something and we're moving on to something else.

"Yes," he says. "Unless you were going with someone else. One of your friends. You know."

Friends, I think. I grin a bit before I can stop myself. My friends. I've been hanging out with Trina and Ashley a little bit. We weren't all planning on going to the dance together. I wasn't going to go at all. They were. I said I didn't want to. They didn't press me on it. I think they are afraid of me. Like if they push me, I'll break. The dance is a big deal. It's like the prom. Above the clock on the wall there is a huge poster, advertising tickets for $10 each.

I remember saying, "Who wants to spend $10 on

standing around and looking at a bunch of kids you'll never see again?" Or maybe I just thought it.

I open my mouth. "Sure," I say. I didn't mean to say yes. I start to blush. "Okay," I say. "That sounds okay."

"You will? You mean it?" He looks all goofy and happy and I don't have the heart to tell him, no, I didn't mean it. I don't know why I said it.

"Okay," I say. "That'll be nice."

I kind of walk away in a daze. I bump right into Dan. "Watch out," he says.

"Hey," I say, then I keep walking, trying to stop my hands from shaking. I go right to Trina's locker and stand there until she shows up. She's late. She always is.

"Guess what," I tell her, trying to keep the nervousness out of my voice. I tap my patch.

"What?" she says. "What is it, Pagan? Are you okay?"

"Boob asked me to the dance," I say.

"You're kidding," she says, smiling. "Are you going?"

"Do you think I should?" I say.

"Of course," she says. "I heard on good authority that he really likes you. Besides," she adds, "I'm going with Caleb."

"You are?"

"Yeah," she says. "I think Ashley is going to go with Dan."

For a minute I feel really hurt, deflated. Like all the air has been sucked out of me. Dan's *my* friend. He was my friend first. My gay friend Dan. He asked Ashley? To a dance? He's not even interested in girls. Then I think, maybe he knew that Boob was going to ask me.

"You know what?" I tell Trina.

"Hmmm?"

"I don't think we should call him Boob anymore."

"Sure," she agrees. "I think you're right."

I feel a little better after that. I may be going to the dance with a goofy boy, but at least I'm not going with a boy named Boob.

I don't cut any classes, after all. I take my gloves off and sneak into class through the back door. The teacher doesn't notice, or pretends not to. Maybe he's heard that I'm crazy. I sit through everything and look around the classrooms and think: *So this is it. This is almost the last time I'll sit here.* I carve my initials into my desk in my last class of the afternoon. It's not the last day of school or anything, but it feels like an ending. There's a glimmer in the air. It's warmer. After this, it's exams.

It's over.

After school, I ride my bike directly to Dr. Killian's office without meandering around first. My bike feels like an extension of me. I think back to the first time I got on, how I slowly drifted off the other side. Now I can ride with no hands. I can balance with no hands and no feet.

Balance. That's important.

I'm early, and I wait outside on the steps instead of going into the waiting room to gawk at the other patients. It's a nice day. It's the kind of day where you want to take off your clothes and gulp the sun into your skin if only it was healthy.

I quit smoking, so I don't have anything to do with my hands. I braid my hair, and then rebraid it again.

Even in a plait, it goes past my butt now. It's too long, I guess. I stand up and walk up and down the stairs a few times. There are only ten steps, so this seems like a stupid thing to do. It isn't enough. I need to do something more. I go to the sidewalk and wait for an imaginary starting gun and I sprint back and forth to the corner. Fast. It feels good. It makes me feel like a little kid.

I check my watch, wondering if I should go inside. Who wants to go into a stuffy little room with plastic chairs and read old magazines? How depressing would that be? I wait until the exact minute of my appointment, and I run up the stairs and into his office. I almost trip, but I catch myself just in time, steadying myself on the railing.

"I think I'm fixed," I say, when I get inside. "Really. Listen, I'm like a normal person now. I'm going to a dance with a normal boy. I have some normal friends. My parents are getting married, so I'll have a normal family."

"Mmm hmmm," he says.

"Really," I insist. "Maybe I can stop taking the pills now."

"No," he says. "No, I don't think that's a good idea."

"Why not?" I'm surprised. I thought he'd be all for it.

"Not yet," he says. He launches into a big long explanation of why I can't just stop, and how quickly I could get depressed again. Just hearing him say that makes me afraid. I don't mean the kind of afraid that makes you scream, but terrified: I feel a sinking in the pit of my stomach. The feathers shift, wings in my belly. Still here, they remind me. We're still here. My throat closes. I swallow, hard. I can't go back to that again. Not now. Not just when I am starting to resurface. I take the paper that he gives me, his handwriting spins off it to the side, inky lace that means something indecipherable. I force myself to breathe.

"I'm going to be okay," I say.

"You are okay," he says. "Don't think you're not."

And so I take yet another prescription to the drugstore.

I'm standing in line when I see Caleb and this other guy from the football team. They're goofing around and being pretty loud. I try to keep my head down, so they don't see me. Maybe they won't recognize me, I think. As though they wouldn't notice a girl with a big black patch on her eye. I pretend to be looking at the shelf of things. Condoms. Pregnancy tests. Fuck, I think. Literally. I laugh a little bit, but I'm blushing. Of course, they see me. I'm not as good at hiding as I used to be. I don't know why that is. I'm bigger, more visible. I've gained weight and muscle and something else. Another dimension that I was missing before. I can't hide.

Caleb says, "Hey, Pagan, what are you doing here?"

I say, "Just picking up some things." There is nothing in my hand, of course. I look around for something. I grab a tube of toothpaste. "You know," I say, "toothpaste."

"Right," he says.

The loudspeaker comes on. "Prescription ready for Riddler," the pharmacist announces.

I know exactly what they're thinking.

"Oh," smirks Caleb. "Picking up some pills, are you?"

The way he says it, I know he thinks they are birth control pills and I wonder if it's worse that he thinks that than if he knew the truth. I wink at him. I can't believe I did that. I winked. Who am I? A person who winks?

"Don't be an asshole," I say. I walk over to pick up

my pills. My crazy pills. Who cares what they think?

"I'm Pagan Riddler," I tell the pharmacist, and he goes to the shelf and picks up the bottles for me, slips them into a bag. Smiles.

"There you go, Pagan Riddler," he says. "All set."

"You bet," I tell him.

I'm at home starting dinner when I realize that the wedding is on the same weekend as the dance. I mean, I should have noticed that before. These are two big events, right? My parents made me check and recheck my schedule so the wedding ceremony wouldn't interfere with anything like swim meets or whatever. I wasn't going to go to the dance, so I didn't care. As soon as I notice the date, my breath catches in my throat. I can't do both, I start thinking. How can I? I can't go to a dance the night before my parents' wedding. I mean, I'll have things to do. I have to help them get the house ready. They're counting on me. They need me. This is how it's going to be: they are having the ceremony in the back yard under an awning, in case it rains. I have to help with the flowers and the food and, well, everything. I mean, they have a wedding person who is helping them, too, but I wanted to do it. Me. I wanted to be a part of it.

Mom's favourite flowers are white roses, so Dad and I have ordered up dozens of them from a big flower shop. It was my idea. I'll have to be home on Friday after school when the delivery arrives to make sure they're okay, to decide where to put them. We are going to be serving barbecued salmon and chicken and a million different salads and desserts. I'm going to make a special cake, with three levels. I was going to spend all Friday night doing that cake. I start to feel panicky with my breathing going funny and my chest tightening up. The wings flap in my mind. Don't panic, I say to myself. I grip the edge of the counter.

The balance, I remind myself.

It's too much.

I can't do it all. I wish Sam were here to help. If Sam were here, we'd probably have a big fight over who was going to do what, but still, it would all get done.

Why did you let go, Sam? How could you leave me to do everything? How can I do it all alone?

A wave of sadness seems to loom up out of nowhere and crashes down on me. As soon as I start feeling sad, I kind of skid down lower and lower until I am crying about Sam again, about how this never would have happened if he wasn't dead. Don't think I don't know that it isn't a very logical thought. It's a crazy thought. Snap out of it, I think. Inhale, exhale.

Eat me, drink me.

I pour a glass of water and try to drink. It sticks in my throat. I can't swallow.

Swallow, swallow, I think. Inhale, exhale, right left. I sit on the floor. The tiles are cool and sticky. A pea pod and some dry noodles are between the stove and the wall. I'm sliding and sliding. I can't help it. It's like travelling down a steep hill with no brakes. Once I get going, I can't stop.

I cry on the kitchen floor for a while. No one is home, so I just sort of lie there and press my cheek against the cool Mexican tiles. They aren't clean. A part of me thinks, I should clean the floor. A dead spider nestles in a web in the corner. After a while, I start to get sleepy.

Everything seems so heavy and impossible, it is all I can think of: sleep.

Not this again, I think.

Oh no, no no no no.

I want to go to sleep. I take an emergency pill and go up to bed.

It's four o'clock in the afternoon and the sun streams through the sheer curtains, but I don't care. The thing is, I can't fall asleep. I'm awake. As awake as I've ever been. The crying stops. I'm all cried out. I lie there until I get too hot and then I push the sheets back.

I get up. Have a shower. I comb out my hair. I feel like I'm maybe half asleep. I have that feeling that I get when I stay up all night to finish an assignment. A detached feeling. A feeling of nothingness. In my hands, the blades of the scissors flash. I hold my breath and I cut. The shears slice through my hair. It falls around my feet like fresh cut grass. My head gets lighter. I cut and I cut.

I cut forever. There is no bleeding. Just hanks of hair covering the bathroom floor.

After that, I do sleep. I dream about Joe and about the piano at the party and about Brett and Daisy. In my dream, Joe is in front of his house and Brett comes out and he says, "My wife." And she is holding Daisy. From inside, I can hear music and in the window, I can almost see the silhouette of Sam.

"Sam," I call, pushing by Joe and Brett. "Sam!"

I wake up, screaming his name. "Sam!"

My voice echoes through the empty house. I lie there for a while, my heart pounding and sweat all over me, before I get up. I make myself sweep the bathroom floor. The hair is heavy in my hands. I stare it, and at my messy cut. It's still long. Still past my shoulders. My head bobs and sways.

I go downstairs. I go into the kitchen and put on a pot of coffee. I stare out the window. Sam, I think. Sam, Sam, Sam. I feel so strange. I just want it to stop.

I wander into the music room. I don't know why. I just stand there in the doorway and wait. What am I waiting for? I pick up the guitar and cradle it in my arms. I pluck it quietly. I'm not playing anything, but I am. There is music.

Then this happens. It doesn't sound true, so I'm writing it down. I swear, while I am playing, I can hear the piano in the background, but I can't be sure. I don't look at it. I'm practically holding my breath. I keep playing, pressing my numb fingers into the strings. I play everything I can think of. I think it is Sam at the piano. I think I hear him. The music is a little jazzed up. It can only be him. The grief inside me stretches its wings and shifts. I can't be imagining this, I can't. It isn't possible.

"Sam," I say. Feathers brush my stomach, my back. A cramp grips me and moves me forward. I can feel blood dripping between my legs.

I don't move.

I know it is Sam.

"Sam," I say. "Don't go."

I hear him sigh. I do. It's like a gust of wind, a puff. And then, he's gone. Soaring. I can feel the air being pushed aside, the feathers forcing his flight higher and higher.

I guess he said good-bye. I guess it was something like that.

EPILOGUE

I pedal hard and then coast down the hill. Inhale, exhale, left, right. Pedal so hard that my feet are spinning and the bike is moving faster than I am. A car passes me and honks. As though I'm taking up too much space. I flip him the bird, but I don't really care. I skim along the pavement, not touching. I close my eyes and feel what it is like simply to move. The tires sing against the road. I don't hear any other sounds. At the bottom of the hill, I brake gently. Pull over to the sidewalk and rest my foot there, waiting for the others to catch up.

The others.

Who are they? I have to think for a minute. It seems strange not to be alone. My heart throbs. I can feel the pulse in my neck, pounding. Others: Trina, Ashley and Dan. We've decided to bike everywhere instead of driving because Ashley wants to lose a couple of pounds to fit into her dress for the dance. She's been on a diet for her whole life, I think. She isn't fat. I think she just likes to diet. It gives her something to obsess about. I mean, we all have our obsessions. Our craziness.

I haven't shown anyone my dress yet. It's on layaway

at the store, and I'm just going to put my final payment on it. I have been making some money doing a bit of housework for people on the street. It sounds pretty lame, but I kind of like it. Mom wanted to give me the money, but I don't want her to. I want this one thing to be something I did for myself. Besides, I like cleaning. I like being able to see into other people's lives. It's cool.

I learn all sorts of things. I learn that everybody's life isn't as perfect as it looks. There's one lady that I clean for who has cancer. You wouldn't know it, unless you saw her on one of her treatment days, when she's sick and doesn't bother with her wig. She's young and pretty. She lives by herself, with a couple of expensive-looking cats. They are a rare breed from Egypt, she told me. They have these amazing yellow eyes. All over her house she has interesting art and sculptures and African masks — things that she has collected on her travels. She has gone all over the world. The thing is, she has no family. She's all alone. Usually, she isn't even home, but sometimes she is, when she is sick. She has no one to bring her a cloth for her forehead, or a cup of tea. She breaks my heart, that lady. Her name is Simone.

I don't want her to die. When I go there, I am always afraid that I'll find her, and she'll be dead. I'm scared that I won't know what to do.

Most of all, I'm scared that I'll end up like her.

Other stuff happens, too, when I work. One day I was at this house I don't usually do. It's Trina's job, actually, she just couldn't make it. I was there, dusting the knick-knacks and enjoying the music on the stereo, when I saw a picture of Joe on the mantle. It was one of my favourite houses. It was modern, with lots of glass windows and skylights, and it had an incredible view of the ocean. The garden was in bloom and there were rose bushes and hedges cut into crazy shapes. The picture was of Joe with his wife. And there was one of Joe with his baby. They were in incredible silver frames, really heavy. I picked one of them up and almost dropped it. I stared at the pictures for a long time. Joe's wife is very pretty. She has a scar over her eyebrow, which, instead of making her look weird, just makes her look better. It's like a perfect flaw. Of course that would happen to her, she would get an attractive scar. She wouldn't lose an eye. Not like me. On the back of the other picture was the name "Samuel Joseph Manelli." It was weird. I never thought of Joe having a last name. He was always just Joe.

It turned out that it was Joe's wife's parents' house that I was cleaning. I didn't tell them that I used to be in love with Joe. I just said, "Oh, I met him once when I had an accident on my bike."

"He's very good-looking," the lady said. "I'm sure you'd remember him."

"Is he?" I said. "I just thought he was really nice."

I like cleaning that house. I traded with Trina for it, after I found that picture. I still like looking at Joe, even though I understand that we'll never be together. He's so happy in all those pictures with his wife and baby, Sam.

We get to the mall and lock our bikes together and I go to get my dress. It's the most incredible dress I've ever seen. It's green silk and it has no sleeves and it crosses over in the front and back. It's also long — it kind of drags along the floor when I try it on without high heels.

It's a good thing that Boob, I mean Robert, is taller than me, or else we'd just look silly together. I get the saleslady to wrap it up in plastic and tissue so that it's protected and then I put it in my knapsack for the ride home. It seems a bit weird to her, probably, that this sweaty kid is buying a really expensive dress and then cramming it into a grubby old backpack, but what can you do. I can't meet everyone's expectations all the time. She kind of looks down her nose at me. I hate people like that. They should just get over it already.

I'm having fun, I realize, when I meet up with the others at the food court. I don't feel crazy. We share some pizza and then go over to the hair place to make appointments for before the dance. I feel like the quintessential teenager. There is just one small shadow in my thoughts, that sets me apart. There is just a faint image of Sam that I carry with me always. I have made-up conversations with him in my head while I sit there, feasting on gooey cheese pizza. I ask him if he thinks he would have ended up at the dance with Trina or Ashley. I always thought he had a crush on Trina, before he died. Then I kind of wonder, maybe he would have gone with Dan. Even if he wasn't gay, he might have gone just to be a friend. That's the kind of person he was.

I think these things, and then I start to get sad. In my head, I talk to Sam. I tell him about the wedding and the dress that Mom is going to wear and the way she hired someone to help her with the Friday night stuff without a blink of an eye. I thought she'd be mad when I told her about the dance. I thought she needed me to do everything.

I was wrong. I don't have to do everything, after all.

I tell him how different Mom and Dad are lately, how even the air in the house seems lighter and less serious. I tell him that the Riddlers are finally going to try to be a real family. The only thing missing is him. Sam.

And I tell him that we'll always be missing him. Always.

I take the long way home, on my bike. I leave the others far behind, and I go up all the hard hills and go all the way around the waterfront, instead of cutting across. I ride and ride. The pavement peels out under my tires like a ribbon. I feel strong and in control. It's hot and I end up taking off my jacket and stuffing it in my backpack with the dress. I smile at people when I pass, and I even stop to pat a dog that's barking at me. I stop instead of running away. Instead of being afraid.

Finally, I get to where I'm going.

The cemetery.

I didn't used to visit. He wasn't really here before. Now that he is, I've planted flowers in a pot on the stone. If you plant them right in the ground, the mowers cut them down. I found that out. The stone is white marble. It's really cool to the touch. Smooth like skin. I sit there for a while, touching it with my hand. Stroking it, the same way I stroked the dog. The stone is still under my touch.

"Sam," I say, and then I start to cry. I will always be crying. I have been crying forever and ever and I'll never stop crying for him. I don't say anything. I cry and pick the weeds that are trying to climb up the stone. I scrub off some moss that is starting to grow. I lie down and cry with my head resting on the marker.

If Sam could see me, he would say, "Get over it already." At least, I think he would.

"Okay," I say. "Okay, Sam."

After a while I start to get cold, so I get up to leave. I am pushing my bike past a bunch of daffodils when I realize I didn't do what I came for. I check around to make sure there is no one else there, and then I change quickly into the dress. The hem gets dirty around the bottom, but I don't care. I change into the dress and then I go and stand in front of the stone and I tell him, "Look. Look at me. I'm all grown up, Sam. I grew up without you."

I'm crying when I say it, but I don't feel sad in the old way. I feel like I'm letting something go. Finally.

I get home and take my pill and hang my dress up so that it will be ready for tomorrow. I can hardly sleep. I'm actually kind of excited. I'm wondering if Robert will try to kiss me. I'm wondering if I'll let him.

The last thing I'm going to tell you about is the film, the film from my camera from the day of the avalanche. When I get home from the cemetery, I take it out of the drawer by my bed and hold it in my hand. It's light and plastic. I pull the film out of the canister and hold it up to the light. It's blank and fogged over, like my eye, but on one frame, I think I can see the silhouette of my brother. My brother, Sam, who died.

I snip that piece away from the rest and press it in between the pages of my journal. The rest, I throw away. It's just junk.

It doesn't mean anything, after all.

ABOUT THE AUTHOR

Karen Rivers has published three previous books: *The Tree Tattoo* (Cormorant, 1999), *Dream Water* (Orca, 1999) and *Waiting to Dive* (Orca, 2000). *Dream Water* was nominated for the Sheila Egoff Children's Literature Prize and was awarded a BC 2000 Book Award. Karen Rivers lives in Victoria, British Columbia.

BRIGHT LIGHTS FROM POLESTAR

Polestar Books, an imprint of Raincoast Books, takes pride in creating work that introduces discriminating readers to exciting writers. These independent voices illuminate our histories and engage our imaginations.

More Books for Teens and Young Adults from Polestar:

Changing Jareth • Elizabeth Wennick
A Canadian Children's Book Centre "Our Choice" book; American Library Association "Pick of the List for the Teen Age"; nominated for the CLA Book of the Year and the Young Adult Canadian Book Award. "A book that is sure to garner the acceptance and approval of teen readers. Highly Recommended." — *Canadian Materials*
ISBN 1-896095-97-6 • $8.95 CDN / $5.95 USA

Witch's Fang • Heather Kellerhals-Stewart
Three teens risk their lives in this high-octane mountain-climbing adventure.
ISBN 0-919591-88-4 • $9.95 CDN / $7.95 USA

Starshine! • Ellen Schwartz
A Canadian Children's Book Centre "Our Choice" book.
"This lively and funny novel is a winner." — *Quill & Quire*
ISBN 0-919591-24-8 • $8.95 CDN / $5.95 USA

Starshine at Camp Crescent Moon • Ellen Schwartz
ISBN 0919591-02-7 • $8.95 CDN / $5.95 USA

Starshine on TV • Ellen Schwartz
Nominated for the Silver Birch Award.
ISBN 0-896095-13-5 • $8.95 CDN / $5.95 USA

Starshine and the Fanged Vampire Spider • Ellen Schwartz
ISBN 1-896095-60-7 • $8.95 CDN / $5.95 USA